T0193109

CAPTAIN WORTHY'S WARSHIP ADVENTURES

William Milborn

authorHOUSE®

AuthorHouse™
1663 Liberty Drive
Bloomington, IN 47403
www.authorhouse.com
Phone: 1 (800) 839-8640

Published by AuthorHouse 05/10/2019

ISBN: 978-1-7283-0481-6 (sc)
ISBN: 978-1-7283-0480-9 (e)

Print information available on the last page.

Illustrations taken from Great Sailing Ships of the World.

This book is printed on acid-free paper.

Acknowledgements

Editing: Terri L. Milborn
Cover: Terri L. Milborn
Research: Terri L. Milborn
Scribe: Terri L. Milborn
Computer Typist: Carolyn Fischer
Final Editing: Carolyn Fischer
Research: Jack Voltz
Research: Chris Schnieder

I want to shout out that I am very proud to be Joseph Worthy, son of the greatest sailing ship commander in the Atlantic Ocean. That commander was Alexander Worthy. His father, Eric Worthy, from the north of England, was also a great sailing ship commander under whom my father Alexander received his training. Eric was the ship commander that commandeered a fortune in gold and silver as a British Ship Captain. He delivered many a prize to England due to the many ships he captured. The British Navy paid Captain Eric much by way of booty on those pirate ships. That, together with half of the booty aboard those ships soon made Captain Eric a very, very wealthy Englishman. Likewise, the officers and seamen became rich after the remainder of the booty was split. By contrast, "The Crown" received twenty-five percent of the booty. Of the remaining, Eric received fifty percent, and the seamen twenty-five percent. That was the standard contract for every captain of the ships-of-the-line.

Captain Eric, my grandfather, contracted with the best shipbuilder in England to build a fantastic four-masted ship. Captain Eric used part of his fortune to create a ship to his specifications. The ship was ready in two years. Eric sold his old ship and applied the funds from the sale to buy new weapons including, muskets, rifles, epees, and cutlasses. He applied another large amount of his booty to pay for his new warship.

The new ship was faster than the Spanish ships or any other existing ship of the time because its' beam was less wide, so the narrow ship had less drag over the ocean water. This new warship will best any ship it will meet in battle. It had cannons that were eight feet in length on the bow and stern, and cannons that were six feet in length on the second deck. In all there were eighty cannons. There were forty cannons on each side of the deck. The cannons had a firing range that was thirty yards longer than any of the Spanish ships or privateers. He had metal plates installed which surrounded the gun ports and the bow, and the four sailing masts. This would create less serious damage to the ship. The extra steel plates were added from bow to stern to prevent cannon balls from damaging his new ship he named Avenger. We could stay out of range of the opposing ships and could still drop cannon fire on enemy ships without their cannon balls reaching the Avenger.

Eric was only able to enjoy two years on his warship Avenger. My grandfather Eric became famous in these two years because of the number of ships he commandeered. Eric was put down by a musket ball and lost his life in a courageous battle with a privateer. Although Eric lost his life, the Avenger won the battle since the opposing privateer was destroyed. He willed the ownership of the Avenger to Commander Alexander Worthy who is my father. Every Worthy captain always passes the ownership of his ship and assets to the next oldest Worthy. This would be my father, Commander Alexander Worthy, who now owned Eric's warship even while he was still commanding a British ship-of-the-line. Captain Eric left his wife endowed with sufficient funds on which to live. Eric's son, Alexander, was viewed as a giant among those captains who sailed warships on the seas. It seemed as if he could control the winds as he pleased and cause the sails to billow. It was as if his new warship was a part of him since he controlled it with such ease. My father, Alexander could tease his Avenger in movement in the slightest of breezes.

Captain Alexander told the Chief Navy Admiral that he would return the ship-of-the-line of which he was captain and promised to use the warship Avenger for missions for the duration of his ten-year commitment as a Navy Warship Officer. The Commander agreed. Terms were agreed upon and he would receive the captain's share of all prizes taken and he would receive captain's wages from the Navy. Alexander, my father, would continue to receive a bonus for each prize delivered to the English shipyards. That bonus would be determined in direct proportion to the value of the ship commandeered. For example, a much higher bonus would be paid to a commandeered four-masted vessel than a three-masted vessel. The Commander agreed to pay Alexander for the use of the Avenger and officer's wages and the same booty that Captain Eric had received.

My father had returned to port when we heard the bad news that mother was dying. We hurried home and found that she had just passed away before we could make her aware that we were there. Father knelt by the bedside and scooped her warm lifeless body to his chest. He laid her down continuing to lay across her upper body. I too knelt by father and held mother's hand and laid across her body. In a little while I felt father's hand and arm creep across my back and pull my body close to his. Soon father stood and pulled me upward and said, "We must go on. We have an obligation to our country and our crew to protect England." At my age of sixteen, this was the worst of times because my loving mother died of consumption.

Father kept our home in Milford Haven, England which he rented out to an officer in the Navy after mother died. Father and I slept in cabins on the Avenger.

On the way to our ship he stopped and turned and said to me, "I am going to make you a member of my crew on the Avenger." I was just sixteen. He said, "Before you are made a seaman you will train and become highly proficient in every single duty that this ship requires to be performed. Joseph, my son, my objective is for you to one day be a captain on our warship in His Majesties Service."

He ordered his Lieutenant Edwards to have his crew to come on top deck where he introduced me to the crewmen. He stated, "This is my son and he will become proficient in every job on my ship. I will punish any crewman or officer who gives him preferential treatment. He is now a trainee being paid by the English Navy. I will, of course, speak to him as a father would speak to his son. Once my son, Joseph Worthy, has successfully completed training I will promote him to an officer. At that time, he will be in charge of training or retraining of all crewmen. When he is considered proficient by myself and functional in each assignment and duty and his demeanor is that of an officer, he will be assigned to myself. Where upon, I will teach him in all skills in commanding and navigating a ship. He will learn how to read navigational charts. He will also learn how to navigate by the stars and also by the sextant and by weather and wind changes.

The ships on this map show where Captain Worthy's warship the Avenger battled and captured Spanish warships and privateers in the southern pirate waters and the Mid-Atlantic. The one circled is the treasure ship. The ships he brought back to the English Naval Yards were prizes for the Crown. The captain's warship was registered as the Avenger, but on its side were large golden letters identifying it as the Annabelle—his wife's name.

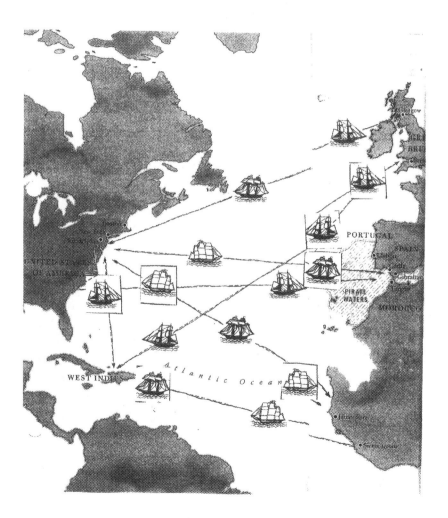

End Seaman's term for every type of rope.

Moon sail-Triangular sail above the highest yard with the point upward.

Full-rigged ship-Originally only a 3-masted square-rigged ship on which all masts were fully rigged. In addition, every ship with more than 3 masts with the same type of rigging. More precise designation: 4- or 5-masted full-rigged ship.

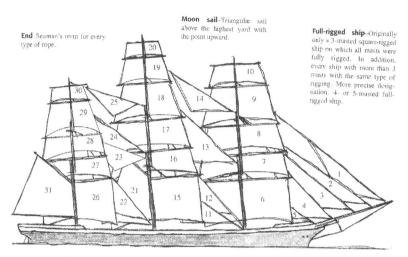

Full-Rigged Ship (ideal rigging)

1. Middle staysail (flying jib)
2. Outer jib
3. Inner jib
4. Fore-topmast staysail
5. Forestaysail
6. Foresail
7. Fore lower topsail
8. Fore upper topsail
9. Fore-topgallant
10. Fore-royal
11. Main staysail
12. Main-topmast staysail
13. Main-topgallant staysail
14. Main-royal staysail
15. Mainsail
16. Main lower topsail
17. Main upper topsail
18. Main topgallant
19. Main royal
20. Main skysail
21. Main spencer
22. Lower mizzen-topmast staysail
23. Upper mizzen-topmast staysail
24. Mizzen topgallant staysail
25. Mizzen royal staysail
26. Crossjack
27. Mizzen lower topsail
28. Mizzen upper topsail
29. Mizzen topgallant
30. Mizzen royal
31. Mizzen sail

Mizzenmast-The last mast on all ships with 3 or more masts as well as ketches and yawls.
Mizzen sail-The sail on the mizzenmast as well as the last fore-and-aft sail on all ships with more than 2 masts as well as on ketches and yawls.

Forecastle-Front superstructure of a ship, reaching from one side to the other.
Foremast-The first mast on all ships with more than 1 mast (but not on 1½-masters).
Foresail-On square-rigged ships the lower sail on the foremast. On yachts the foremost sail set next to the mast (the stayforesail).

Mainsail-The lower sail on a full-rigged mainmast or the sail on the mainmast in the case of a fore-and-aft rig.

Gun ports-Openings in the side of the ship through which the muzzles of guns protrude.

Fore-and-aft sail-All sails that run parallel to the length of the ship.
Halyards-Ropes with which yards or sails are hoisted.
Halyard winch Winch with which yards or sails are hoisted or lowered.
Hawse-Round or oval opening in the side of a ship or in the deck through which lines or chains pass (for example, an anchor hawse).

Keel-The backbone of the hull. On wooden ships a beam that runs along the center of the bottom of the hull. The floor plate is attached perpendicular to the keel and supports the frames.

Hulk-The hull of a retired, unrigged ship, often used for storage.
Hurricane deck-Continuous deck above the main deck. The bulwark reaches to this deck, producing a continuous superstructure.

Poop-The rear superstructure of the ship, extending from one side to the other.

Planks-More or less wide boards that are attached to the frames in the case of the body of the ship or to deck beams in the case of the deck.
Lower sail-The lowest square sail on a full-rigged mast (foremast, mainsail, etc.).
Luff-The forward edge of a fore-and aft sail.

Mainmast-The second mast on a ship with 2 or more masts (but not on a 1½-master).
Helmsman-The person who stands at the wheel and steers the ship.
Hoist-To run up a sail or a flag.
Lateen sail-A triangular sail that is set on a lateen yard (something in between a yard and a gaff). It probably originated in the Mediterranean.

6

Quarterdeck–An elevated portion of the main deck in the rear of the ship.

Railing–The "fence" running around an open deck.

Rake of mast–Downward slope of a mast or masts. Allows the masts to sustain a higher wind pressure.

Rabbet–Grooves running the length of either side of the stem and keel into which the planks are fitted.

Reef–The part of the sail that can be shortened (to shorten is "to reef"). The reef runs parallel to the yard or to the boom.

Reef points–Small lines that are attached to the bottom of a sail in one or more rows with which the sail can be tied up.

Rig–The sails and masts of a ship considered as a whole.

Royal(-sail)–A single square sail that is set above the topgallant sail(s)

Run (day's run)–Distance covered by a ship from noon one day until noon the following day.

Running rigging–All ropes that are used to operate sails and to move the yards, gaffs, and other spars

Gaff–The upper spar of a gaff-sail. The lower end clutches the mast from behind like a fork.

Jacob's ladder–The ladder to the top of the top of the topgallant mast.

Patent anchor–A stockless anchor that can be partially retracted into the hawse.

Shrouds–Ropes of the standing rigging that support the masts and topmasts on the sides

Skysail–Simple square sail that is set above the royal.

Lee–The side of the ship that is toward the wind.

Log–To measure the ship's speed from on board.

Full sail–The condition of a sailing ship when it has set all available sails.

Sloop–1. The rigging of a boat with 1 mast, a mainsail, and a forestaysail. The most common rigging of recreational vessels. 2. A 1-masted freight vessel (also a "jolly-boat").

Snow mast–Light lower mast that stands aft of the mainmast.

Sound–To measure the depth of the water.

Spars–Round wooden pieces on board except for masts and topmasts.

Spencer–A gaff-sail without a boom.

Spinnaker–A large, light, balloon-like sail that en route is set with the true direction of the wind anywhere from dead astern to about abeam.

Spritsail yard–On older sailing ships a yard that is attached below the bowsprit.

Port–The left side of a ship.

Port lids–Flaps that cover the gun ports from the outside on old warships.

Stability–The ability of a ship to right itself from a horizontal position.

Standing rigging–All of the ropes and cables that serve to support the masts and top masts and that are not moved

Starboard–The right side of the ship.

Stays–The ropes of the standing rigging that support the masts and topmasts in front.

Staysail–Any sail that is attached to the stays.

Mizzen boom–Boom of the mizzen sail. On a large ship it usually extends above the stern rails.

Stem–More or less vertical extension of the keel on the front and back of the ship.

Stern–The back end of a ship.

Stern gallery–Often richly ornamented, balconylike structure around the stern found on many old warships and also on many trading ships

Stock anchor–A very old type of anchor. The stock is fastened perpendicular to the main shank.

Streak–Usually white-painted band running around the otherwise black-painted hull at the level of the row of the gun ports in order to highlight (or give the impression of) the ports.

Studding sail–Sails that square-riggers set in light, rough winds. First the studding sail spars are pushed out to lengthen the yards, and then the studding sails are set on the studding sail spars. Very rare nowadays.

Tack–On triangular fore-and-aft sails the front corner of the sail. On square sails, depending on the placement of the sail, the lower front corner.

Tiller–A horizontal lever running along the ship with which the rudder is turned. On large ships replaced by a rudder wheel.

Topmast–Extension of the lower mast that can be raised or lowered. Large sailing ships often have two topmasts, the topmast and the topgallant mast.

Tonnage–Measurement of a ship's cargo-carrying capacity (a measurement of volume and mass).

Top–Platform on the mast that rests on the crosstrees.

Topgallant–A single or double square sail that is set above the topsail (or topsails) on a square-rigged mast.

Topsail–General term for the square sails on square-rigged schooner (topsail schooner). On fore-and-aft schooners the

Jibboom–An extension of the bowsprit. In contrast to the bowsprit itself, the jibboom is designed to be removable. In many cases the jibboom can be further extended by an outer jibboom. This causes the staysails to be farther apart, better utilizing the power of the wind.

sails above the gaff-sails (gaff-

Jib-headed sail–Also called a Bermuda sail. A high fore-and-aft sail with no gaff, the head of which reaches to the mast top.

Tramp–A commercial trading vessel that picks up cargo wherever it happens to be rather than following a regular trade route.

Transom stern–A flat back end of a ship (as opposed to a round stern).

Trim–1. Trimming is the process of putting the ship into a good position (through proper setting of the sails, proper positioning of the cargo on board, etc.). 2. To move cargo from one spot on board to another.

Trireme–A Greek galley with three banks of oars.

Trysail–A fore-and-aft sail on staysail schooners that is set between the stay and the mast in front of it.

Warp–The forward movement of a ship in which, with the help of a kedge and of the smaller warp anchor, the ship is moved from one anchoring place to another.

Windlass–A winch with a horizontal axis.

Yacht–A sailing vessel that is not used for commercial purposes but rather for sport, recreation, or out of love for sailing.

Yard–Spar perpendicular to the ship's length axis on a mast to which a square sail is attached.

Yard-arm–The end of a spar (yard, gaff, or boom).

Between deck–On large sailing ships, usually only a single deck between the main deck and the bottom of the ship.

Bilge–The lowest point in a ship, in which all water that has leaked in or all water that has formed through condensation can gather.

Bilge keel–A humplike keel on the bilge of the hull in order to reduce rolling; often found on large, flat-bottomed ships.

Fisherman's staysail–A light sail whose head is attached to the top of the main topmast and whose tack is attached to the cap of the foremast.

Laid up–Temporarily taken out of service.

Aft–Toward the back of the ship.
Awning deck–*See* hurricane deck.

Bachstays–Stays for the masts and topmasts that stand aft of the shrouds.
Baldheader–Square-rigger, usually 4-masted, with no royals.
Ballast–Material added to a ship in order to achieve an optimal stability (for example, sand, stone, or water). Especially important on voyages without cargo.
Bark, or barque–Originally only 3-masted square-rigged ship with 2 full-rigged masts and the last mast with a fore-and-aft sail. In addition, 4- or 5-masted square-rigged ships, which except for the last mast with its fore-and-aft sails rigging have full-rigged masts only.
Belting–Particularly strong layer of planking on wooden ships. It rises above the outer skin, stabilizes the ship, and prevents damage during docking.
Davit–Gibbetlike crane on which boats are hung. Davits always occur in pairs.
Deadweight–The cargo carrying capacity of a ship (deadweight all told), whereby provisions, etc., that the ship needs for the voyage are included.
Deck beams–Beams supporting the deck that run perpendicular to the hull and rest on the frame heads.
Depth in hold–A vertical measure taken in the hold. Upper edge of the floor plate to the lower edge of the deck beams (uppermost continuous deck) midships.
Depth to deck–Measured at the ship's midpoint from the bottom of the hull to the upper edge of the deck beams of the uppermost continuous deck.

Boom–A round piece of wood to which the lower edge (foot) of a fore-and-aft sail (for example, a gaff-sail) is attached.
Bow–The front end of a ship's hull.
Bow ornamentation–When there is no figurehead, carved scrollwork or baroque fiddleheads often adorn the bow.
Bowsprit–A spar that is firmly attached to the body of the ship that extends forward above the stems. The forestays, to which the staysails are attached, leads to the bowsprit.
Bowsprit topsail yard–A small yard to which the bowsprit topmast is attached; a small mast that stands on the bowsprit or the jibboom. Primarily on old warships.
Brace–Rope with which the position of a yard with respect to the ship's axis is changed. It is attached to the end of the respective yard.
Brail–To haul a sail up to the yard with the brails.
Brails–All parts of the running rigging that serve to haul a sail up to the yard or gaff.
Brig–A square-rigged ship with 2 full-rigged masts.

Carvel build–Build in which the external planks lie next to each other such that a smooth surface results.
Chain plates–The metal fittings used to connect the shrouds with the outer hull.
Clew lines–The two brails that lead to the clews (lower corners) of a square sail.
Chocks–Structures for storing boats on deck, adapted to the shape of the boat. Also used to store rope.
Classification–Every larger ship is placed in a "class" based on the way it was built, its level of safety following its construction, and in what condition it is maintained.
Clinker build–Build in which the external planks overlap each other like shingles on a roof.

Displacement–The amount of water displaced by a ship.
Dolphin striker–Downward-pointing iron or wooden spar mounted below the bowsprit to spread the jibboom stays.

Bulkhead–A dividing wall that separates one part of the interior of a ship from another.
Bulwark–Solid wall surrounding an open deck.

Cap–Spectacle-shaped fixture at the point where the mast and topmast (or two topmasts) are connected.
Capstan–A winch with a vertical axis.
Crow's nest–A protected platform on the mast used for lookout duties.
Clipper–Sharply built, fast sailing ship of American origin. Later and currently a general term for a fast, large sailing ship. Even 4-mast barks are referred to as clippers.
Coamings–Raised edge around hatches and at the thresholds of doors to prevent water from entering.
Cringles–Iron or wooden rings around masts or stays to which staysails are fastened.

TO BECOME A CREWMAN FIRST CLASS I HAD TO KNOW ALL THE TERMS AND MEANING OF THE TERMS ON THIS AND THE PRIOR TWO PAGES. I ALSO HAD TO LEARN HOW TO USE ALL THE SHIPS' ROPES, SAILS AND EQUIPMENT MENTIONED IN THE GLOSSARY OF TERMS.

It is up to you, my skilled seamen, to move his training along quickly, but do not pass him along to the next job before you personally can attest to his skill level in that duty. I will personally ask you to commit to that task. You must guarantee me that he is skilled in a task that you have taught him.

If I feel that he is competent in all the many duties required on the ship, I will then recommend him to the Navy of His Majesties Service for further training at the Naval Academy. Once his academy training is complete, I will expect him to be appointed as a captain of his own warship on one of the ships-of-the-line. I will finish by saying, do not forget that he is nothing more or nothing less than just a trainee at this time and will receive no special treatment. Son, stand beside me so all of the crewman can see and recognize you. At this time, everyone of you have more skills than my son. He is the lowest of all of you in terms of knowledge and experience. It is totally up to you to train him well. I expect no less. An award for excellence in training will be an extra ration of rum for those that trained him in a specific skill. I said to myself, "Well, that speech is one I will never forget, and in some ways may live to regret."

Many of the seamen aboard my father's ships were young, whiskerless faced and inexperienced lads like myself. Other than that, the men were of all different ages. The old bearded, grizzly, weather beaten faces were the most skilled and interesting of them all. Mostly, they spent a lifetime on a ship at sea and for many the sea was their home. This was their choice to always be at sea rather than on land.

Just so you know how hard it is, I will tell you one-by-one all the jobs I have had to learn and the good and bad experiences. I suppose the hardest thing I had to learn is the purpose and use of all the ropes and lanyards of the ship. Every one of the ropes had a precise purpose. I needed extra time to learn that job of ropes and ties. I also learned and became proficient in making knots and the ties that were used in the various ropes to control the sails. These knots included: The slipknot, bowline, square knot, blockwall hitch, carrick bend, clove hitch, cat's paw, figure eight, granny knot, overhand knot, fisherman's bend, half hitch, reef knot, turk's head, sheet bend, timber hitch and sheep shank.

I had to learn and use the halyard winch to raise and lower the sails. I learned especially the use of the mizzen mast which is the last mast of the ship. The sails were different and so was the use of the winch in the task of raising and lowering the sails. My trainer often became aggravated with me at my apparent slowness to learn.

I was to learn the use of the backstay which holds the top mast and the mast in place. The Sail Master was one of my trainers and had taught me all of the names and terms of the sails and duties required to employ them. This (confidentially) I had trouble learning and remembering. I made an outline of these sails and the names for them which I will show in these pages. I will also include a listing of parts of the ship and what they are for. I heard Captain Alexander Worthy comment to his Lieutenant that the next time we were in port he wanted the belting, which prevented damage to the ship, either replaced or repaired. I knew my training instructor told me that the belting stabilizes the ship and rises out of the outer skin of the ship and prevents damage during docking. One nasty job was to oil the connections of the yardarm and masts so that the sails and the ropes wouldn't rot.

I was shown the bilge and was told its purpose which was to hold the water at the lowest point of the ship and would have to be bailed out by buckets.

I learned quickly to climb the rope ladder to the fore and aft sails and adjust the ropes on the boon which is attached to the winch below. This is where I had my first injury. I scraped a good part of my skin from my fore arm when it was caught between the ropes and the yardarm. I learned to secure the stay sails which are attached to the spar which is attached to the main body of the ship—bowsprit. I was afraid I would be injured again. I was told by my sail master and my trainer that every rope has a reason and every seaman aboard had to learn all that I was taught about the sails and ropes. I felt that these specialists providing the training were extra hard on me because I was the captain's son. People think working as a seaman on a ship is a job for simple people. Not true! It is a skill without which you could die in battle by the guns of a privateer, including the many Spanish ships whose purpose is to defeat us. It is too much here to write about all the sails and names and their purposes, so I am putting that important information and diagram in the book.

There was the procedure of weighing and hauling in the ship's anchor. I also had to learn to use and load and fire the cannons in sequence. There were eighty cannons that had to be secured on the rails or the ship's movement would cause the cannons to do damage to the ship's hull. Securing the cannons on their trunnions was important, as was opening the outer ports when needed which was also a duty when firing was expected. Our new style of trunnion had the ability to have a range of firing upward or downward as the enemy ship approached our broadside.

While climbing the rope ladder to reach the sails, as many other crewmen have done, I became afraid of falling as I crawled out onto the yardarm and helped drop or raise the sails. This was done al all three levels of the mast. This was treacherous when the ship was rolling back and forth and up and down under high seas. The ship would be heaving and rolling in all directions. I have seen a crewman named Chester fall to his death. Others that fell received broken limbs. Bravery, dexterity, and knowledge were all required to do this job. I had to ride the look-outs crow's nest. It was the only time I had suffered from motion sickness. Many times, I spewed a meal onto the deck below. I still cannot manage the sway of that crow's nest without becoming sea sick. Keeping a look-out for other ships and relaying the sighting as well as ringing a bell when a look-out spied a ship could be key to survival. Only a few seamen had the ability to recognize the type of ship approaching and relay to the deck Lieutenant as to whether if was friend or foe. As yet, I have not achieved that skill.

Working in the galley below and preparing meals for the crew was good duty. My galley training included preparing trays of food to be delivered to the officer's dining area which was in Captain Alexander's cabin (or quarters). My father, Captain Alexander, had his officer's briefing everyday at meal times. Occasionally, my job was to deliver food to these tables. Father would look at me and give me a wink. That one wink made me feel loved and that he was with me and for me!

I can't forget the swabbing of the deck – a daily ritual. We would clean it whether it needed it or not. By every rail of the ship there were wooden buckets. Each bucket had a long rope attached to it so we could dip water from the sea. There was a barrel of lye soap from which we would take a portion and a brush and get on our hands and knees and scrub the deck. We all had calluses from this ordeal. Many of the crewmen, unassigned to a job for the day, would do the same. From the bow clear to the stern, we would dip into the several buckets and clean and drop them onto the deck where the water would roll from the deck back into the sea, just as waves do. We would then go to the second deck below and do the same, except there we would have to swab and wring out the mops.

The training included would be assisting the forty cannoneers in leveling the cannons on the trunnions under strong supervision of the armory officer. We would clean the barrel of the cannons as well as the outside. We would help sharpen the knives. There were swords and epees which were stored in the armory as well as those that needed servicing. This was done daily just to be sure all weapons were sharp and ready to fight with. I would then help the English deck fighters clean the many muskets and clean the barrels and make them shine. I would help see to it that all body belts and straps holding muskets and knives were ready to put on quickly. We made sure that each were ready and could hold two muskets. The cannoneers and deck fighters were the best my father could find for his ship. My father, Captain Alexander, was the only captain to have selected a crew who were skilled fighters in the use of weapons. They were called his warrior crewmen. Each of them was worth two men in battle. We required the warrior crewmen to train every day so they could be at their posts and ready to fight within less than four minutes.

Two cannoneers assigned to each cannon would aim and fire the broadside of the enemy vessel as it came into bear. They had better aim by adjusting the cannon up and down in the trunnion. After firing that volley, cannoneers would go to the opposite side of the ship and perform the same procedures when the captain brought the ship around to the opposite side of the enemy.

Mostly due to the ability of the cannons, we had fewer of these kinds of battles. Our new type if cannon could reach about thirty yards further than the enemies.

During training there was no actual firing, but all were trained in shooting in succession. While the cannoneers took a new position on the enemy and a new round for another broadside shot, we would take that time to reload. The same process was followed on the other side of the deck when the other forty cannoneers would be doing precisely the same maneuver.

Of the two men assigned, one would load and aim and the other would fire. As soon as the enemy ship came into bear they would fire. I, too, was trained at this discipline, as well as the seamen, in the event that any of the cannoneers were injured or killed in battle. I actually participated in several sea battles. When an all-out ship-to-ship broadside battle occurred, every crewman on board would take part in the action. Every crewman would be given muskets loaded and ready to shoot. Each had two muskets and were given powder and two additional musket balls to be loaded as needed.

Probably the most important part of our training was fighting, both for our lives and our ship! Almost every encounter would require some fighting. There were some ships we attacked that would give up without a whimper and would run up the white flag – indicating NO BATTLE!

Another duty was to work as a scullery person in a small area where we washed equipment, and pots and pans. Feeding one hundred crewmen would mean a lot of food and a mountain of pots and pans to clean.

As a seaman, one of my most important duties was to be one of the four look-out men who would search the horizon for ships that we could go after, or might be coming for us. Only the officers had spy magnifying scopes to view the ships at a distance, or what was happening on board one of the ships near us. The watch was from bow to stern, port side and leeward side of the vessel. In all, there were four look-outs posted. The watch was twenty-four hours a day. Every eight hours there was a change in the watch. If anyone was found asleep during watch, they would feel the pain from the "cat-of-nine-tails". They would only be given one week to heal after the punishment. I have seen this penalty many times. The crow's nest look-out position was the most important because of the 360 degree of ocean that could be observed.

Another never-ending job which I had to learn was to fill the many ship's lanterns with whale oil. I did not have to learn about the brig or the infirmary. But the officers showed me where they were located. When we had to clean the barnacles from the bottom of the underside of the ship, the captain would pull the ship broadside to the shore, and wait for the tide to go out so the vessel could tilt seaward and the crewmen could get to and clean the bottom, or devil, of the vessel. Everyone worked at this job so we could be back on board when the tide came in and righted the ship. We could then sail to deeper waters. After this job we all had to re-sharpen our knives.

The last training area was to receive instruction in all the ship's laws. For these, I had to memorize and repeat them to the officers.

Finally, after three years of training and taking part in a number of sea battles, I was happy to hear that I would be recommended for a promotion. I made close friends with many of the crewmen. When one of them died in battle the officers would inform the others.

Captain Alexander announced that every seaman could have a ration of rum for I had successfully completed my training. The sixteen ounces of rationed rum was in honor of this event. The barrels of rum were placed on deck, and every man drew his ration of rum from the barrels. We all then drank and enjoyed our rum. It was then that I learned the biggest lesson of all. I went to one of the two kegs of rum from which all of the crewmen drank their ration and drew myself another cup. Many seamen saw what I had done. There was a rule that a ration of rum was to be only one. Rum, like all other commodities on board was rationed to last for the duration of the voyage.

The next morning there was a notice given for all crew members to come on deck immediately. The captain stood on the bridge and said, "Trainee Joseph Worthy – step forward and address yourself to the captain." I thought, "Why, is this my promotion?" Captain Alexander said, "Trainee Worthy you are guilty of breaking a ship's rule by taking an extra ration of rum." I heard every seaman mutter and murmur.

Captain Alexander said, "You will receive two strikes from the cat-of-nine-tales immediately. Take your shirt off and stand facing the main mast. An officer will bind you." The officer for provisions had reported that he saw Joseph take an extra ration of rum. He did not challenge Joseph or stop him from taking that rum. Therefore, Officer Brighton, you will give my son two lashes of the "cat".

After I received horrible bites from those leather straps on my back, I remember feeling blood streaming down my arms and back, and the pain was so great and intense that I could barely stand it. The two strokes of the "cat" left eighteen whip marks all of which drew blood. I still have these scars and remember the lesson.

The captain walked down the steps from the bridge and he said, "Unbind my son." He wanted to confront me face-to-face. We looked at each other for a long time. I could see tears welling up in his eyes. Trainee Worthy, you have successfully completed your training and have also been promoted to Seaman First Class. You are promoted to an officer and will assume the duties of Officer Brighton. Office Brighton, you will assume the duties of the armory of weapons, and ammunition and the brig area. The captain continued, "Officer Houseman, your duties will now be to observe all crewmen on both decks and see that they are performing their duties. You will also look to the condition of the equipment. Anyone who is not performing well will lose their ration of rum, spend time in the brig, or feel the "cat" depending on the violation."

I spent two days in the infirmary after being seen by the doctor. Then I took over my job as officer in charge of food, water, rum--- and commodities!

It was a little over a year at this assignment that I was requested to come before Captain Alexander Worthy. Finally, I thought, "Is this the promotion or am I in trouble again?" I went to the Commander's cabin and I stood in from of him and his three lieutenants and he said, "We agreed you should be a Lieutenant of His Majesties Service. You will be assigned to me to learn the profession of commanding a warship. My First Lieutenant Skinner is presently in charge of navigating by sea charts and announcing the ships direction. You will train with him and myself and learn how to navigate by the stars and by the sextant. You will learn to make changes according to storms, wind and other weather. I will carefully observe your training in these skills. You will take quarters which are currently used as a storage room under the bridge. We have prepared the room for you. You will join myself and the other officers for all meals. I was elated and could not keep from crying. My father sidled up close to me and whispered in my ear, "son, officers of your position cannot cry or show emotion in front of anyone. It is a sign of weakness." We drank a class of rum that the commander had provided for all the crewman in honor of this occasion. In fact, he allowed us two glasses on that special day.

I was proud of my father who was known to be the most skilled Captain of the seas. It was about two years ago when he went to battle with a pirate ship. I was standing near my father when he took a musket shot into his chest. The force of the shot knocked him backward into my arms. He sank to the deck while I was trying to hold him up. He called out, "No! Not yet! No!". I felt his pain. He looked into my eyes and said, "Be brave, you are now the Master of this Ship. I will be joining your mother now." It is confirmed in the Captain's Book that this ship is now yours!" He murmured his last words, "Son, I love you..." He closed his eyes and I felt him drift away. He looked at me for the longest time. I heard a small gasp as life left him. His body was still warm. He was gone...

His lieutenant carried him to the infirmary where he was prepared to join his other shipmates who were to be delivered to the sea. His lieutenants, as customary, gave me his uniform which they folded in linen. They placed him on the burial board and covered him with the British flag which was attached to the board. The next day all seamen were present when my father slid from that burial board into the sea. Before the sea burial I stood by the burial plank and embraced him as he had embraced my mother Elizabeth when she passed away at our little house. I wept on the British Flag on which my tear stains would remain. His lieutenants folded that flag and gave it to me as the custom was then, and so it is now. My first lieutenant looked at me with tearful eyes and said, "You are now Commander Lieutenant Worthy and we will be proud to continue our service under your command as we did for your father."

I directed the ship be turned and re-routed to the Irish Sea to Milford Haven, England. It took two weeks to make that journey and I stayed in mourning for at least a week, until I became aware of my responsibilities.

Lieutenant Skinner commanded the ship, per my orders, during that period.

I strolled up and down the deck, and the men looked at me as if I were my father, for we looked so much alike. Two nights prior to entering port I brought my crew together and I said, "All the crew, in honor of my father, are free to have two rations of rum. You may drink this tonight and tomorrow before we dock. You may have no more than two rations of rum. You remember why I have those eighteen scars on my back. However, you are not to drink if you are on duty, or in a skirmish or in a battle with another ship. I do this in honor and respect for my fathers' voyages. After we dock, I will give all crew members land time for two weeks. Remember there will be payment of bounty for the ship we are taking back to England. Officers, you will be sure that everyone receives partial pay and be here on the day before we go to sea again. Lieutenant Skinner will meet with me daily. I will keep you informed of our new orders."

My father, Alexander, received this ship from his father Eric, who was also killed in battle at sea. This ship, like so many other ships, was owned by the captain that commanded it.

The entire crew and myself continued to mourn for my father, Alexander, as we sailed south into the Irish Sea. We finally pulled into the English port and moored the ship at a deep-water dock in Milford Haven. The Navy had an elaborate ceremony in Milford Haven for Captain Alexander. Everyone was there. The streets were filled with the many people and seamen who either knew or went to sea with this famous captain.

The Royal Navy recognized the loss of the great Captain Alexander Worthy, and his years of service as a ship-of-the-line captain. I was contacted in person by a Navy Admiral from the Royal Navy Office. He said, "The Navy accepts that you have the right and authority, and position of captain of the ship that you own. You will not be required to study at the Royal Academy for we know of your training and fighting experience you had under the guidance of the great Captain Alexander". He brought a contract which both he and I signed. He said, "This Navy contract states that the same conditions will prevail that Alexander and his crew had with the Crown. The same sum of payment for the use of your vessel will apply that you father had received and will be placed in your account every six months in the Bank of England. You will receive a monthly sum for your service as captain. That payment will be placed in a separate account for you to draw upon at your pleasure. You will also be allowed to keep one-half of the gold and silver bullion that you take from Spanish ships or privateers. Your crew will receive one-fourth of the bullion captured and one-fourth will be given to the Crown. Before anything is divided, England will receive their share first. This will hold true for any Spanish, French, or privateer ships that you may do battle with. Any ship you capture will be brought back to an English Navy Yard, along with its entire cargo. Your crew will be paid by England's H.M.S. Navy. The pay will be in accordance with the rank or position that they have on board the ship. This agreement will be honored for ten years."

This would make me, Captain Joseph Worthy, the youngest captain of all the ships-of-the-line. I was treated with great respect for they knew my father, Captain Alexander Worthy, had taught me how to command a ship and do battle.

The Navy agreed to assign security to stand guard to prevent anyone from coming aboard my ship while my crew and myself were taking land time. I have given myself and crew freedom to rest and prepare for whatever assignment I would receive from the Navy.

During the next week, I met with all of my crew and some other crewmen from other ships that were there to be considered for duty aboard my ship. My lieutenants will take part in these interviews. If crewman from other ships did not like their current captain or would like to sail under my leadership, they will be considered. I signed on the best of my crew and a few crewmen from other ships that I knew to be excellent in the many positions I had to fill. I picked as my First Mate, Edward Holly, a battle officer who had once captained his own vessel. I filled every position, apologized to the rest and said, "Maybe next time!" Then added, "If I have vacancies in the future, I will put posters out and consider you!"

That evening I stayed aboard ship and planned how I would spend my time. The next day would be one for the memory books. At dusk I decided to go to a pub called the Bounty. I had heard from my officers that it was a great experience. Near the north end of the port along side the docks, the Bounty was permanently secured. It sat broadside to the pier. It was a famous old Spanish warship that the English Navy had commandeered. I thought It was large and beautiful with its four masts. The Navy felt it would be too expensive to refurbish. The Navy removed all eighty cannons that could be salvaged for use on another English ship. The crippled ship was close to Milford Haven port where it was brought and moored broadside to the dock. The Navy just left it there because it felt it could not make the journey to the Navy port. Here is where the Irish family, the O'Hara's, purchased it from the Navy for a mere token of its value.

Top side there was a string of lanterns firmly attached to the top sail masts. I approached the broadside of the ship where there was an extra-large door on which was painted the skull and crossbones. There was a ship's steering wheel from the helm. I turned the wheel and the door sprang open. At that very moment as I stepped onto the floor of that massive second deck, I felt a body which had been pushed backwards into my front side. I found myself in the midst of a seaman's birthday ceremony, where the one having the birthday was pushed from seaman to seaman for a big hug. They were all shouting and laughing. That is when "Billy the birthday boy" was pushed into me.

Like my father, I was an imposing figure. They saw me, the six-foot, six-inch, broad-shouldered man with black hair and piercing green eyes standing before them. Some were awe-struck at my appearance. All the crewmen started laughing and said, "Who is this well-dressed giant of a Navy captain coming to our party?"

I slowly scanned the faces and eyes of all the seamen that were around me. It is strange that looking into the eyes of these men could create a change in mood. I quietly looked at them. Everyone of them caught my eye and I said, "crewmen, my name is Captain Joseph Worthy. I was commanded by my father, Alexander Worthy, who was killed in battle with a privateer less than four months ago. He won the battle but lost his life. I heard I could come here and that this place would help relieve my depression." The music stopped and there was silence all over the huge deck. I could hardly call it a deck. It looked more like an elaborate Spanish dance hall, bar and stage.

The silence was broken when a crewman yelled, "Since when to Navy men of rank associate with crewmen?" I quickly said, "Gentlemen, at heart I am still a crewman. I am skilled in every single solitary job there is to be done on a large war vessel of His Majesties Service.

A crewman yelled, "Have you ever stood watch on a crow's nest?" I said, "You can ask any of the crewmen about the times I have spewed a meal on those standing on the deck!" A few laughed. That was encouraging.

"Sir, have you ever climbed a rope ladder and dropped sail?" I slipped off my waist-coat and hung it on a chair and rolled up my sleeve and bared by scars. The scars were from my wrists to my shoulders and they were from that duty. I told them that I got the scars from those ropes. I showed them all including their girlfriends who were present. I felt that they were leaning toward friendship with me.

"Sir, have you ever been a cannoneer?" I replied, "Seaman, I have planted many a cannonball into the broadside of an opposing ship, and I have seen a number of the cannoneers and their cannons demolished by an enemy cannonball."

"Sir, have you ever participated in a battle on top deck?" I asked, "Your name seaman?" "My name is Timothy." "Timothy, I'm not proud to tell you that during my three-year training I have fought in at least eighteen battles on the sea. I have shot many a musket ball into the body of an attacking crewman who was out to kill me. Also, my sword has crossed the shoulders and back of an enemy officer. You know that this is the reality of war at sea. If you are proud of killing another seaman or officer, then shame on you! Remember every man who has pledged to fight, it is not because they want to, but it is because they are required to." Again, stillness and quiet prevailed.

"Sir, have you ever swung the 'cat-of-nine-tails'?" I paused a good long time and removed my shirt. I turned my back to them and said, "Not yet. I have not, but I felt the sting of those tails." All present looked upon my scars left by the "cat". There were many.

"Gentlemen, before you ask any more questions. I will tell you that I worked bailing out the bilge and I worked as a scullery, and assisted cooks delivering meals. I've loaded supplies. I was also present when my father, the captain, was killed by a musket ball, and I was by his side when he was buried at sea. I have seen many other crewmen who were my friends buried at sea as well. I mourned them all and so should you. Please compare yourself to my experiences and ask yourselves to accept me as a fellow crewman."

There was a stillness and then suddenly a roar of applause and yelling to show that they accepted me. The seamen's apparent leader said to me, "Sir, you are now honored as a captain in our crew." I said, "I presume you will now allow me to have a shot of rye and whiskey with you and a ration of rum and a tankard of beer, and enjoy your company?"

The senior crewman said, "Henceforth, you will never pay for any drink you receive at the Bounty. We will all chip in and take care of that charge." I said, "Thank you, but no! I will always pay my way and occasionally buy you a stein or two. Now get on with your party! I apologized to Billy for interrupting his birthday.

On the opposite side of the Bounty was the longest sit-down or stand-up bar I had ever seen. The bar was made up of a series of oak decking brought in from scavenged ships. They stretched from the aft to the stage. The barstools were from the commandeered Spanish flag ships. Unique were the carved engravings that were present on the bar top and front,

At the entrance to the bar station, were the barrels of rum, kegs of beer, and displayed whiskey were stored on a shelf behind the bar and underneath there was a center gate and two gates that could only be entered from either end. From the storage station you could make your choices including Irish Rum, English Beer, Irish Whiskey, Jamaican Rum and French wines. Irish Whiskey was the most prevalent choice because of the Irish O'Hara's. The family owned the Bounty. There was a stage which extended out onto the second deck. The barkeep drew our drinks and received our coin. I asked, "Where is the owner gentlemen?"

"Sir, here I am! I am Annabelle. I am a performer here at the Bounty. I manage the Bounty for my father and mother who own the pub." I looked up where she was standing and I asked, "Where were you throughout all those questions?" She said, "We entertainers have a space in the backstage area, but I was sitting just backstage listening!" I said to her, "I have never seen such a beautiful lady with such bright curly red hair. You are beautiful Annabelle!" The crewmen applauded and drank to that. She walked down from the stage and walked up very close to me, practically nose-to-nose and said in a loud voice, "You are beautiful too!" Then added "Thank you for joining us! We are so fortunate!" She stepped to a place in front of the stage and took a chair at her special private table. Remember I said that the large stage took one fourth of the space on the second deck. It had been enlarged to allow for performing.

Above the second deck stage there were captain's quarters on top deck that were converted for the entertainers to change and rest before performances. From there was a small stairway down to the second deck stage. A large curtain separated the backstage area from the large front stage where the entertainers performed. Annabelle raised her eyes and said, "Entertainment for this evening will now begin!" A portion of the curtain from backstage opened and revealed a number of musicians and they started playing an Irish tune or two which Annabelle sang to. Then they played an Irish jig and performers came out to front stage and danced several wonderful Irish dances. Then four Irish cloggers came to front stage and the other Irishmen retreated and now the musicians played music to which Irish girls and three Irish men could do clogging! Straight they stood---hands by their sides---while their lower legs and feet did a fancy bit of clogging to the music.

We all applauded for those that did the Irish jig and the clogging at the conclusion of their act. The dancers, along with those doing the clogging, retreated to backstage to the stairway which led to the captain's quarters on the top deck.

A real hit was an Irish lad that sang "Danny Boy". During that song beer sales doubled. He sang three famous Irish songs and then went backstage to the stairs and climbed the stairs to the captain's quarters for the entertainers.

Annabelle announced, "Your entertainers have to go home to their families. Are we not happy to have them? They will be back tomorrow night." Then everyone cheered. Annabelle then announced, "Now for the act you have been waiting for! The ladies you are about to see are four of my very best friends. Treat them with much respect for they are about to reveal in dance much of their bodies which many men are not accustomed to seeing. They will perform two French dance routines. They will also do a French version of the "can-can". Oh, how they can dance!"

When all the entertainers left, Annabelle stood alone on stage, then sat at her spinet and played and sang so beautifully some Irish love songs. She had even the most rugged seamen crying in their beer. She finished and there was a roar of applause and she said, "I will see you tomorrow!" Then she just waved and came down the steps from the stage and walked to her table. She sat and slipped off her shoes and put her elbows on the table and her chin in her palms and closed her eyes.

At the end of the singing and dancing, I raised my cup to all and with a cheer in my voice I said, "God Bless you all!" I went to Annabelle's private table and I said, "I see that you are resting. May I Interrupt you and sit with you?" She said, "Yes, sit with me!" I said, "Annabelle, I have been to sea a lot during the past four years and have only been ashore a few times. I have not seen many women, and have not been to many pubs, but I have seen enough to know that you are the loveliest lady I have ever seen. Would you consider having dinner with me and walking with me tomorrow evening?" We will walk on the boardwalk along the dock and we will get to know each other a little better.

Annabelle said, "Thank you, I will". I said, "No, Thank you!" I said, "I am looking forward to tomorrow!" I turned and went toward the door of the Bounty while the crewmen patted me on the back. As I was going out the door, Annabelle said, "We will meet at my home just across the road." Later I discovered that on this beautiful, starry and moonlit night the music would play and they would dance on the top deck with the sails billowing overhead and the lamp lights glowing. They would be dancing and romancing.

I arrived at Annabelle's home early the next evening and was greeted by her father. He looked up at me, his mouth opened and his eyes widened as all people do when they first meet me because of my height, looks and stature. I said, "I have come to meet with your daughter. Her singing at the Bounty was delightful. She seemed to control things that were going on at the pub. Is she more to the Bounty than a singer?" Annabelle, standing by her father interjected, "I am a caretaker along with my brother Aaron O'Hara of the Bounty whose owner is our father and mother. Aaron has the same responsibilities as I do since neither of us can be there the many hours that the Bounty is open. We take off times according to our personal lives.

I asked, "Your name sir?" He replied, "Mickey O'Hara." At that time his wife came to the door and said, "I am Anne O'Hara." She too looked up- at me and was astonished! My stature seemed to be a major attention getter. Everyone always asks, "How tall are you?" My reply is always "Six-foot, six-inches more or less and 50 inches around the chest." It was not just jy height but the broadness of my shoulders. Now you must know that this was an awkward moment. Anne continued to look into my face as she led me to a plush chair that seemed hand hewn. I asked, "May I presume you are Irish Sir?" He said, "On yes, my name is Mickey and you know my last name----O'Hara, and this is my bonnie lass Anne!" They both reached for my hand. He took my right hand and she took my left, and not only welcomed me but pulled me into their parlor. Annabelle looked at us and said, "I am so proud to present a captain of one of the Crown's Warships and my friend for the evening."

She than added, "Joseph would you mind staying here this evening and having dinner with us? Mother has prepared her wonderful Irish stew." I said, "A good choice." Annabelle turned toward her parents and said, "You must know that just a few months ago Captain Joseph lost his father in a warship battle at sea. Joseph's father was shot during a sea battle with a privateer. I brought him here to cheer him up and keep his mind off of the tragedy that befell him." Anne then said, "Oh Joseph, we are so sorry for your loss. Only those who have lost someone that was dear to their heart can know that feeling. We will talk of this no more."

I sat in the chair and Mickey said, "I made this chair and the other furniture. It is a hobby that I pursue when the Navy is not calling on me to repair weapons." Anne said, "Yes, they have contracted with me as well to make officer's uniforms and occasionally to make repairs on sails." She approached me, leaned over and said, "I noticed you have a ragged spot on the waistcoat of your uniform…" She came closer to me and said, "I can take that stain away and mend that jagged hole so you will never know they were there." I said, "Oh, I will always know they were there." She looked up into my eyes and suddenly knew the emotion she caused and what that jagged hole meant. I looked down into her eyes and nodded. She knew because she had repaired many a uniform such as mine. While looking into my eyes Anne reached up with her palm and covered that place and said, "Okay Joseph, I understand. I will finish dinner now. We both know that stain and musket ball tear will never be repaired." I could see she was embarrassed. I said, "It's okay Anne."

Anne mentioned that Mickey and I should get acquainted. I thought this would be easy to do because I happen to notice that on his work-table he had pistols and two muskets on which he was making repairs. All of this being a ship commander's responsibility, I asked him many questions about what kind of repairs he was making. I picked up the pistols and not knowing they were loaded pulled the trigger and shot a hole in the ceiling. Anne came running from the kitchen and screamed, "what happened?" Mickey just laughed and said, "We can fix that." I could see that Annabelle was embarrassed. I asked, "Could you invent a safety device to prevent the musket from firing accidently? Too many men are accidently shooting themselves in the foot. In fact, apply this to the rifles as well. If you can do this, I will help you patent the idea with the British Patent Office. It will make it so that no manufacturers can sell a weapon without a safety device." Mickey said, "What a brilliant idea! Why did I not think of that?"

Anne soon summoned us to dinner. It was great to get away from seafood and have a nice Irish stew. During dinner I, for the most part, was just eating and nodding my head to questions they would ask and I would occasionally answer.

At the end of the evening, I bid the family farewell and told them it was the best evening for me of the entire year. I said, "You both impress me so much. I am honored to know you and it was an exciting evening wasn't it!" Annabelle stepped outside the front door with me and I thanked her for a wonderful evening. I asked if we could do this again. She replied, "Oh yes, tomorrow night you are invited to another of mother's wonderful meals. We will have corn beef and cabbage. On another evening, I will arrange with my brother Aaron to take responsibility for the Bounty and then we will take our walk on the dock as planned."

Those were splendid days we had on those walks along the boardwalk. There was hardly a bench that we didn't sit on while we had long conversations about her past and mine. I could talk about those conversations we had over the following the days that I spent with her family and on those long walks, but I won't, because that narrative would take too long. We carved our names on the benches on which we sat. Now I want to tell you about that tenth day.

It was the best evening a man could ever have to make a proposal. Yes, there was a full moon, many stars and a warm breeze. I suspect Annabelle may have guessed that I might be proposing that evening because of my demeanor. We sat on our favorite bench that had a view of the sails against the starry skies. I held her hand. I turned to her and gazed into those lovely Irish blue eyes and asked, "Will you spend the rest of your life with me?" She said, "Oh Joseph, I would love to, but it is the biggest decision that we will ever make. I want to say yes. I would love to say yes, but I need to know your answer to very important questions. First, I must continue to be a caretaker of the Bounty as does my brother Aaron, and also take care of my parents and the entertainers. I have promised my parents to take care of the Bounty and for our financial independence. I also feel responsibility toward all the dancers and other entertainers of the Bounty. We would have to find other ways to meet my obligations in order for me to marry." I said, Positively, I agree!" She said, "I wish to continue with what I love to do so much, which is to sing and play the spinet at the Bounty." I said, "Yes, we will work that out with your friends. We will make this work!" She then said, "Where shall we live since living with my parents in their home is something that the Irish do not do after they wed?" I said, "Yes, Annabelle, my father has given me, as his will states, a home that I have here in Milford Haven. It is where I now live. The home will be equally shared when we marry." I added, "It's where I was raised and it is now where I live when I am not at sea."

She smiled at me and said, "I will, Joseph….I will marry you….be my commander! We will marry as soon as we attend to the things we have discussed."

Right then we sealed that life-long promise with a long embrace ending with a kiss. Annabelle said, "Oh Joseph, one more thing, will you ask my parents for my hand in marriage and together we will tell them of our plan. My father and mother will want to make wedding plans at our catholic church." I said, "Of course!" I leaned toward her and placed my fingers in her red curly hair that topped that pretty Irish face and gave her a long loving kiss. I continued gazing into her eyes and said, "Do not worry about your future if I am lost at sea. Everything I own you will inherit and that includes a small fortune that I have in the Bank of London. Probably the most important question would be, will you have a child with me? She said, "Marrying and having children is something I have dreamt about for as long as I can remember, and now that dream can come true. Yes, I would love to have children with you!" I said, "I have no experience in the bedroom. I would need some help there." She quietly spoke, "Me too! But I am sure we can figure that out together!" I smiled and said, "What if your parents say no?" She said, "Not likely!" I said, "I have one final question." Annabelle said, "No, not another question!!" I answered, "Will you allow me to place your name in large gold-tinted letters on both sides of my ship? You will have your name on the finest warship ever built! It will replace the name that is there now – the Avenger."

She looked at me and jokingly said, "I'll have to think about that!" To his amazement, she then smiled and laughed and said, "In a way it will be like marrying your ship too!" I said, "I had not thought about it that way. You will be marrying me as well as my warship!" She said, "Yes, it would be an honor to have your ship named after me."

We immediately went to her house and rapped on the door. I said, "Mickey and Anne, I am going to marry your daughter." Annabelle said, "No, Joseph, you must ask them, not tell them!" Her parents said, "With all our blessings, yes!" They were overjoyed with the thought and I said, "Don't worry, my future Dad and Mom, I will see to it that all of Annabelle's obligations to you and the Bounty are met."

Finally, the big day had come. All the arrangements were made for Cardinal John to conduct the ceremony at the Bounty. I did not know I had so many friends and acquaintances until I saw the number of Navy men of all ranks attend the wedding. Along with Annabelle's family, there were also many friends of the O'Hara's. The ceremony was solemn, but at its conclusion there was an abundance of food, drinks, and merriment both in and outside of the Bounty. It was a grand excuse for all to have a good time and it lasted for two days.

I looked for Aaron and he was pleased when I threw my arms around his shoulder and said, "I hear that you too have found a lady. I am happy to be your brother-in-law. I hear that she is and Irish girl and a friend of Annabelle's."

Annabelle and I moved our belongings into our fine little home that my father willed to me. With all the gifts from the wedding, you could hardly find a place to stand or sit. Annabelle said, "I am thrilled in seeing the beautiful things and how the rooms are furnished. It will be a great place to raise our children." We had a three-day honeymoon before the Navy officer came knocking on the door.

The officer came to the door and said that I was to immediately, with haste, go to my ship and meet with the Admiral. I said, "Annabelle, I am sorry. I will see you later." A messenger was sent to tell Annabelle to send my locker of belongings back with the messenger. When I reached my ship, the Annabelle, my lieutenants had already contacted all my seamen to bring their gear to the ship and that we were going to sea immediately. In fact, all provisions, including munitions were already on board and ready for us to attack a Spanish warship. On this very day, years ago, I had just experienced the death of my father. I trembled at the thought because of my responsibility to Annabelle, my wife, and my ship the Annabelle!

On arrival at the ship the Admiral ordered me to take my warship Annabelle and find and attack a Spanish warship that had recently sunk one of the ships-of-the-line that had fewer cannons then the Spanish ship. I was commanded to patrol the British Channel for one year to defend the country against invaders. At that time my ship would be replaced with another and I could return home.

I did, indeed, find that Spanish warship and a cannon battle ensued. The battle continued for a brief period until we finally won by toppling its major sails including its center mast. The Annabelle is known as a ship that could stay just out of reach of cannon fire but be able to reach the opponent's ship with our cannons fired from a greater distance. It took only a few hours to bring down that ship and those masts. Even then, we were swifter than they in maneuverability.

They too could alter their position causing this to be a major battle of cannon fire. We fired upon that ship until its captain rose its flag showing defeat. We took the ships captain aboard and put him in the brig. All the other crewmen aboard that ship surrendered their weapons. Every crewman on that ship was told to remove their shirts and take the cannonballs from their cannons to our top deck and store them in wooden barrels. This was procedure. The Spanish crewmen were told to stay on the second deck and they could have one blanket during the trip back to England. Some of the crewmen were injured, but no one was killed on either ship. We would have lost many men had there been a ship-to-ship broadside battle. Because of the maneuverability of our ship, we were able to sustain a distance that would prevent death and injuries from happening.

I, Captain Joseph Worthy, and crew brought back a large Spanish warship as bounty for England. It was a grand victory. I took the enemy captain's ship and its crewmen to a southern Naval yard in England. The victory was proof that Annabelle was able to maneuver successfully at sea and fire cannons at a long distance with accuracy. I replenished supplies of all kinds oand we headed back to the English Channel.

It was twelve months to the day, when we returned to port Milford Haven. What a celebration awaited us. The news of the conquest preceded us on our homecoming. The Chief Admiral that sent us was there to welcome myself and my lieutenants. He asked that the chief cannoneers come forth and they were honored by the Admiral. He said, "Captain Joseph, your records will note this capture and you will be recognized for further promotions." After a night of rest, we went to sea again.

No sooner had we sailed to our channel, we were again accosted by a Spanish four-masted warship. This time we took refuge in the fog. We raised all sails and ran like hell from that monster ship. It was not the right time or the right place to engage in another battle with that Spanish ship. We had just finished a battle that brought injuries and we were not in a mood to engage in another.

I did not feel we had completed our mission when we came back from that one-year assignment. We came back to Milford Haven licking our wounds and wanting revenge. I moored at the dock and told everyone to go home until further notice. As agreed, security men were there to watch the Annabelle until I received further orders. I was overtaken with sorrow when I reviewed the damage done to the deck and side of the Annabelle on the previous battle. The men we lost in the battle will be forever on my mind. These are men who I have been to sea with for many years.

I said, "Admiral, I have two requests." He asked, "Yes, Captain Worthy, what are they?" I replied, "I wish to take the Annabelle and my crew on a voyage to Ireland where I will load up the ship with as many cases of Irish whiskey and barrels of rum as I can to supply the Bounty Pub and retain as many cases of whiskey and barrels of rum to be used on the Annabelle in the next few voyages. Sir, when I return have a wagon ready and I will load your wagon with a bountiful supply of a great Irish whiskey and some rum, at no charge to you!" The Admiral put on a smile that extended from ear-to-ear and said, "Have a successful voyage captain!"

Joseph said, "Sir, I have one more request. Will you permit this crew thirty days land time when we return? I will pay them their wages and you will not owe me anything for those thirty days. After a year at sea they have a lot of activities and business to catch up on. I will be ready in thirty days from our return. Then myself and crew will await further orders." The Admiral stated, "All of this is acceptable. I will have several important voyages for you to undertake as the master captain that you are, along with your notable successes at sea on your fine warship the Annabelle."

Then I left for home. When I got to the door of my home, I thought I would knock on the door to surprise Annabelle. When she opened the door, it was I that was surprised, for in her arms she held the biggest baby I had ever seen. It had to be a Worthy! I did a little jig in expressing my joy. This not something a captain of my station is ever seen doing. Annabelle said, "Please may we name the baby Will? It expresses who you are because you have the will to succeed in all of your ventures." I said, "Of course, where there is a will there is a warship!"

We spent the rest of that evening telling each other how the last year went. She said, "My friends at the Bounty helped me so much before, during and after the baby came. Mom and Dad have been spending so much time here you would think that they lived here. Mother loves your place Joseph. I said, you mean our place." Annabelle said, "In every way it has a woman's touch." I said, "Of course, it had my mother's touch and now yours to make it so pleasant." I added, "Annabelle, you can't believe the major battle I had and I want to tell you all about it. I would like to describe this battle that we had with the Spanish warship."

I cradled the two-and-a-half-month-old baby in my arms and just looked at him and held him high in the air and continued to stare at him. I murmured, "Your mine! Your mine!" I leaned back in my chair. I must have fallen asleep right there. When I awoke Annabelle was getting ready to go to the Bounty to work. I told her, "I don't care—not tonight!" She said, "Okay, I will be right back. I have go to tell Aaron to take over. We are going to need a third manager." Annabelle put the baby in his crib and left. I leaned back to rest a little longer. Well, you guessed it, Annabelle found me in a deep sleep when she returned. She just let me sleep.

The next morning, I felt cheated for not having my evening with Annabelle. I returned to my ship and gave orders for the crew to be on deck for my announcement. I said, "Men, we are going to Ireland to pick up as much Irish whiskey and rum as we can hold on the Annabelle and when we return and the ship is made ship-shape for the next voyage, you will all receive 29 days land time and on the thirtieth day I will receive new orders from the Navy which will take us on a new adventure at sea. You will all be given a substantial portion of our share of the booty tomorrow. I am sure you would need that sum for your family and to pay debts and have a good time. By the way, I have a baby and his name is Will Worthy. Someday, my son will be a captain of the English Fleet. My lieutenants will advise you precisely when to pick up your well-earned share of the booty. We will leave for Ireland after the ship is loaded with provisions for our voyage at dawn. Check in with your superior to find out when we will weigh anchor. Don't be late."

I returned home to tell Annabelle about the next voyage to Ireland and its purpose. Then we went to her father's home. I said, "Mickey, I am about to make you a happy man!" He said, "No, don't tell me its another baby on the way!" Joseph said, "No! I have received permission to go to Ireland to stock the ship with as many cases of rum, whiskey and beer as the ship will hold. When we get back, we are going to store cases of Irish whiskey and rum in the lower deck of your pub the Bounty, which will last for a long time. We will also stack barrels and kegs in your workshop." He leaped up and down as if he were doing an Irish jig.

The next morning at the break of dawn, I kissed little Will and Annabelle goodbye. The crew was ready to go and I called to them to remove the ropes from the dock, raise the sails and head to sea.

It was a wonderful lazy, easy going trip across the Irish Sea. It was nice for all of us to think that the purpose of this trip was not to attack or be attacked…we hoped! The wind was brisk and the sails billowed and I think we set a record for the fastest time in crossing the Irish Sea. It was very early in the morning when our crows nest scout bellowed out, "Land Ho!"

It was a very foggy early morning as we crept into the mouth of the port. I could not believe my eyes when, through the fog, I saw a huge four-masted Spanish Galleon docked there. This could be a dream come true if we could take down that galleon and bring home whiskey too. It would hold a lot more whiskey and rum than the Annabelle could hold.

I told my lieutenants to contact every crewman and tell them not to even whisper or light a lamp as my lieutenants and I were planning the taking of that ship. All of the men were given arms and told to be stealthy and make no noise and do not load their weapons until they were told. NO NOISE! NO NOISE! NO NOISE! The man who gives us away will meet the "cat".

I had two of my skiffs lowered and manned them with my best seamen warriors. Our warriors quietly rode the skiffs to the side of the Spanish ship where they quickly boarded. They found no Spanish lookouts on the top deck. They then flashed a lantern in our direction. After our skiffs were returned to us by two seamen, we rode back to the enemy ship. We stealthily boarded. Apparently, the entire Spanish crew, including the commander, were celebrating in a huge pub on the dock.

I said, "Load your weapons men. Warrior crewmen follow me." All of us stormed into that pub as fast as we could with weapons drawn. I told them, "Don't shoot unless shot at. We don't want to create a shooting combat. You listen to my orders when we get in there. As we rushed in the door of the pub, I said, "Get on hour knees immediately!" I told them to place their weapons on the floor. I told my men to look for any box or crate in the back room to put the collected weapons in.

I told the seamen of the Spanish Galleon to place their weapons (knives) in those boxes. From the center of the group I suddenly heard, "I am the sheriff. I thank you! I cannot control such a group and they said they had just captured a pirate ship loaded with treasure." I said, "All of you---on the floor! Officers and captains know that I have commandeered your vessel and it is now bearing the English flags!" I continued, "If I return you to England you would be treated as pirates and hanged or jailed. I will not do this for I look upon you as doing your duty for your country as we are doing for ours."

Joseph continued, "You have taken a job for seaman's pay and now I offer you Spanish crewmen to be crewmen on my ship the Annabelle, or stay on your own as a crewman where you will be paid double the pay Spain is giving you. Only those of you who can understand and speak English will be considered to be crewmen of my ship, the galleon, or the pirate ship that I am commandeering as well. Those of you who can speak and understand English will now be escorted to the pirate ship under guard led by my next in line Lieutenant John and several warriors and a couple of my officers. Lieutenant John, start right away and ferret out the men who qualify to be your crew or are worthy to be among us."

Joseph said, "Take more of the crewmen who do not qualify to the skiff and on to the pirate ship and take them and distribute them to the several fishing ports on the west coast of Ireland. Be in haste! Get it done and hurry back here with the minimum crew you may have kept from that pirate ship." Joseph asked Caption Salvador of the galleon, "What have you to say?" He replied, "If I had met you on the high sea, I may have bested you and the Annabelle. But we will never know." Joseph replied, "You would not be captain of a grand four-masted galleon if you were less than exceptional in our business."

Joseph told Captain Salvador to join his crewmen who could not speak English and that Captain John will take them to the pirate ship that they had just lost. He indicated that Captain Salvador would also be dropped off at a port of his choice. Joseph said, "Now crew and Captain John and warrior seamen and officers make this happen now. I expect you back in two days. You are to go now!"

Captain Salvador asked Joseph, "Instead of shipping me to west Ireland, will you permit me to be your lieutenant navigator? This will allow your lieutenants and mine to sail all three of those warships to the port in England. You must never let it be known that we were crewmen of the Spanish ships!"

Captain John freed the captains of the captured pirate ship and the crew and part of the galleon's crewmen to three different ports along the Irish coast where they continued life as seamen.

The best of the seamen can be easily hired by the many Irish fishing boat captains along the Irish coast. I am enlisting lieutenants and officers from among the most skilled or you, and the rest we will leave with the sheriff, so he and the other men of this city can place you. This is Sheriff O'Malley's job. I am going to expect you to work with the sheriff on this project.

Joseph said, "I will pay the pub owner for all damages done and drink consumed during that celebration. I will reimburse those who had injuries for which they needed a doctor from many of you who are bleeding from your fighting and hell raising. You see my warrior seamen are standing along the wall, and in the center of the room, in case anyone of you need guidance in my orders. I see that my crewmen have found empty cases of whiskey in your store room."

Joseph said, "Those of you who want to be hired by me, step forward and my other armed crewmen will guide you to my ship. Until interviewed you may sit on the top deck until we see who could be qualified as experienced crewmen. Those not selected will be led back to the pub. Whoever is not placed as crewmen for my ship or placed by the Irish sheriff, will ultimately find placement or even to back to Spain. We count One hundred twenty-five of you in this pub.

Everyone—all one hundred twenty-five of you---sit next to each other in rows starting by the bar rail on the other wall facing the seamen. I have a table where I and my lieutenants will sit. We will interview each one of you one-by-one." The interviews proceeded until nearly dawn. There were fifty that met our needs as each were qualified by two of my officers. For those not qualified, they would remain in Ireland to find their own way. They will be released and at the mercy of the government and in Ireland's custody.

I then interviewed the Spanish Captain Salvador who was quiet and friendly and answered all my questions. I said, "What did you do with the pirate ship's bounty?" He replied, "I transferred it all to my quarters and my officers' quarters. I have not had time to value it but I know it is a vast fortune. I know you are trying to decide what to do with the officers and crewmen from my ship and on the pirate ship and set them free. Except for enough crew to sail the galleon, they really have no value to you. I would expect if, I were you, to have the cannons on the pirate ship rendered useless. Since they would have no ammunition or weapons for the cannons, therefore it would be helpless. It could go to one of the Dominican Republic's islands to make a new start." I said, "Hell no, we have captured that warship and we will keep it just as you have done. I have offered seamen from your ship and the pirate ship an opportunity to be on the new crew for the galleon if they qualify for the pirate ship. That ship and the galleon will be under my command. Those men that we keep must understand and speak English as you do."

He answered, "I have no allegiance to Spain. I only work for them---doing their will! Would you allow me to be placed on your crew? I would be able to apply my skills to any need you have." I replied, "You may be lieutenant and my navigator as you requested. You will have no authority to give orders, but I will pay you a navigator's wage. I will place my current navigator as captain of your ship. Some day we may enter a port where you may wish to leave my service and I would agree to that. In return for that favor, I ask you to review the seamen we select and advise whether you think we have made a bad choice and suggest who would better serve me on the ship that you will now be navigating.

Lieutenant Salvador, I will pay you the same that I now pay top wages for the navigating job, and for a change for you, it will be an honest wage working for England---your enemy! Go to Lieutenant Goodson and tell him he is to give you two sets of English Lieutenants apparel. Throw your current apparel over board." Captain Salvador replied, "I am a mercenary and will work for whoever pays me the most, which is why I was a captain on a Spanish ship."

I made changes in the crews selected and my Lieutenant John is now wearing captain's clothes and taking command of the galleon with an understanding he is to follow my orders and directions. Everyone on all ships will wear an English uniform.

I sent out word up and down the coast that I am buying whiskey, rum and beer. Since I have done that, coaches and wagons have been arriving at port and I have purchased the goods. I had them loaded onto the deck whereupon my crew has placed the crates and boxes on top of, and in front of, the chests of booty that lined the walls in my quarters and my officer's quarters. This process of buying went on all night. I smiled at my new Lieutenant Salvador and said. "It looks like you are going to share in the booty after all! Because you too will receive a share of booty from any ship we capture." There was no return smile.

Those with horses can earn good pay for their use, but you must contact every distillery and maker of Irish whiskey, beer or rum. I will buy on the spot all the product that they have. All of those who have brought buyers will be paid a bonus. And the buyers will be paid a fair price for their product plus a bonus.

We want this process to move fast. I will have more than one pay-master ready to pay you. Do not overstate the value when you fill this four-masted galleon with barrels and boxes of whiskey, rum, rye and beer. Then you will put the galleon out and bring the Annabelle in and you will fill the storage area of my ship. Tell us if you are not paid and we will, as I promised, give a bonus for that person who has contacted you. By the end of that day every bit of whiskey that I bought was on the dock and aboard ship. My ship Annabelle will be well on its way soon. "I, Captain Joseph Worthy, promise you that I will patrol the Irish Sea in the Annabelle that you see in the harbor. I will on occasion visit you to determine if you have any more marauders."

On the fifth day on the dock stood the many people that we made promises to. My accountant and pay-master and two lieutenants began dispensing Spanish gold and silver coin as promised.

Somehow that Irish pub had become alive again. The Irish pub looked like new and we could see many of the newly enriched crewmen heading straight away to that pub. Its swinging doors never stopped flapping open and shut as crewmen entered the pub to put down celebration drinks. The last order of business was the off-loading of whiskey and rum from the many carriages and wagons that one-by-one stopped at the gangplank. They came in from every where to off-load onto the Annabelle and the Spanish galleon, and store whiskey and rum and beer on board them. It took until high noon before all was off-loaded onto my ships. The whiskey and rum were stored on the second level of what was once a Spanish galleon. To have stored all of this on the top level would have imbalanced the ship. We paid more than the actual value of that whiskey and rum. All were happy.

We finished our business there in the afternoon. The crew on each ship was greatly reduced but we felt we had sufficient crewmen to make the voyage back to Milford Haven. God forbid we have a skirmish with a privateer!

I directed the treasure warship and the Spanish galleon to be anchored in the harbor. I will take that ship as an additional prize back to England. The crew from that ship will be allowed to join our crew since they are merchant men. I will have one of our lieutenants be in charge of that third ship, including its navigator.

It was late that night before all the whiskey, rum and beer was stored aboard all three ships. Nevertheless, as tired as the men were, we departed from Waterford Port with the treasure ship, the Annabelle and the galleon. We had to provide the crewmen to operate all three ships. I wondered how it was that the pirate ship had acquired a four-masted galleon. I mahy never know.

Everyone is paid now. I will offer any experienced Irish seamen to sail with me for good pay. I was so fortunate because I was able to hire seventy-five able-bodied experienced seamen before we departed early morning the next day. I placed thirty men on the galleon, twenty-five on the Annabelle, and twenty on the treasure ship. I saw to it that they were immediately trained on firing the cannons.

For security we will follow the galleon and keep the treasure ship to our port side. Thereby allowing us to maintain fire power over both vessels. Lieutenant Skinner maintained the ship. I have enough cannoneers to provide firepower to port, aft, and stern areas of the sea.

I am sure that any privateer that had an eye on us reconsidered with wonderment on seeing three four-masted warships heading toward England.

It was a good breezy afternoon during our crossing. I had sent my pay-master and lieutenants to get a better count of the gold and silver stored on this galleon. They came to me as I stood on the helm of the Annabelle and said, "Sir, never have we seen or heard of so much gold and silver that we have stored on both ships, the galleon and the Annabelle." I said, "Do not say too loudly but whisper to me what you have found!"

The pay-master replied, "We cannot determine the millions that there are on gold and silver coin and bars. Of course, this coin when converted to English pounds would be a greater amount, which cannot be calculated without making conversions. In brief, it is beyond belief!" I said, "Gentlemen, do not breathe a word to anyone one on our three ships of what we have come upon. Such an amount of money would induce a mutiny even by our own people!"

During the balance of our trip, we lived in the glory of our booty. Basically, this would be enough money for everyone to retire. My Lieutenant Skinner's navigation was doing great in handling that four-masted galleon. I let him lead the way as we followed close behind. Captain John was doing well on the third ship which was the pirate treasure ship. At last, I heard from the crow's nest, "Land Ho!" And also heard the bell ring. A new set of problems entered my mind since the amount of money based on past settlements was so great, the Navy Commander and the English Crown might deem this would be too great an amount to bestow on myself, Joseph Worthy, and crew. One-half of all gold and silver would be too much for one command captain. One-fourth of the balance would indeed be an enormous reward to give to the seamen. I'm sure they would be elated to receive the remainder of the total of the gold and silver coin and bullion. What to do?

I cannot move cases of whiskey and barrels of rum to the Annabelle on the open sea. I will have to stake my English contract claim and stand by it. After all, they would be receiving this great Spanish ship as bounty, as well as the rest of the valuable cargo. The second problem was if we were to bring this great four-masted ship into the harbor some may wonder if the Spanish were bringing the war too close to home. I therefore ordered our British flags to be posted on top of every mast, on the bow of the galleon, and the third commandeered ship—the treasure ship. I am seriously thinking of mutiny. I am quietly thinking it may be time for this discussion but my first plan is to keep it all a big secret for a few years and that I keep these three ships to patrol the Irish Sea and the English Channel. If this is not allowed, then I will make a decision to take my ships to sail west.

The fifth day my ship the Annabelle and the galleon sailed out of Waterford port on our way back to England. It was a rough trip home and even the best of the seamen had motion sickness. We were about a month out of that Irish port when Captain Salvador of the galleon said to me, "I am the better man and a better sea captain than you. You were lucky in the taking of my ship and you did <u>not</u> win it in battle. I have never sailed a sailing warship as sleek and fast as this."

One day, while I was standing near the bow, my helmsman called out to me, "Look out captain." I turned and saw Salvador strike with his epee and slash open my shirt and flesh on my upper arm. I nearly fell overboard in trying to recover myself. My own epee was in my hand faster than I knew I could unsheathe it and quickly warded off a second strike. The crew and lieutenants gathered around in my defense and I said, "No, this is my ship and I will defend it on my own." I was told later that this duel between myself and Salvador lasted longer than anyone expected. We both had slashes on our upper body with blood drenched shirts. Blood was smattered all over the deck and rail. I was in pain and felt a surge of anger. In one great strength of fury I screamed at him, "It's over Salvador!" Then I impaled his upper chest and heart to the hilt. He stood and gazed at me in the trauma of dying and held fast to the rail. With his last breath he cried, "I'm sorry Maria."

I stepped forward, yanked my own epee from his chest, and hugged him. I held him against the rail, kissed him on the cheek and said as he was taking in his last breath, "I am sorry but it had to be. I will see to your family." I could feel his nod and I heard him gasp and I gently let him go overboard. I never saw a may crying and dying at the same time.

As he slid backward on the rail, he left a blood trail right over Annabelle's name on the side of the ship. As he disappeared into the sea, I yelled out, "Poseidon, I send you a seaman to present to Neptune!" I turned and stood erect facing the sea and said, "Carry on crew!" Then I let my officers help me to the infirmary.

The ship's doctor stitched me up. I did not lay in recovery, but stayed at the helm next to my helmsman where I held the ship---Just Annabelle and I gazing out to sea!

For most of the voyage my scars healed and I announced, "I will be my own navigator on the rest of the voyage home. Lieutenant Skinner, you have dreamed of being a navigator of a warship, so here is your chance. I will teach you on the way home. I am still weak and need someone to man the wheel and navigate a good part of the time."

I could tell that my crew was proud of me and showed it in every way. I later heard that some of those grizzly old seamen cried when they saw the compassion I had for an enemy captain. I felt, on that day when they witnessed that bloody duel, they would take a fresh look at the opponent they had to fight and sometimes kill.

It is always a grand sight to reach port Milford Haven. My temporary Captain John was told to get back into his lieutenant's uniform and return to his navigation job. Half of the Spanish crewman that I hired requested permanent positions. The other half wished to leave. I paid them well and away they went. Now I have three ships (warships) at my command. The two additional ships I acquired followed me into port. They were named the Horizon and the Neptune. They had individual wooden letters made and painted and placed on the sides of the front now of both ships.

At the entrance to the harbor we sent a small boat ahead and told them to make accommodations for docking the four-masted galleons. Except for some other crewmen on shore, most of the town's people had never seen three four-masted warships or could dream of their size with all of their extra cannons. I sent a skiff to shore with orders that the ships already docked there must move elsewhere. We reached our docking spaces and moored our ships with ease. We moored the Annabelle as close to our pub the Bounty as we could get. The sails gleaming in the sunlight over Milford Haven will be a sight that will probably never be seen again.

I looked down the ramp and saw my wife Annabelle, with baby Will in her arms, come running to meet me. Her mother, father and brother Aaron were right behind. Mickey eyed me and said, "Captain, what did you do?" Annabelle said, "Tell us all about your trip!" I said, "I will after I get hugs and kisses from my bonnie-good-looking Annabelle!"

I looked at my family and said, "I have work for you to do immediately. Lieutenant, I want you to go with Mickey and Aaron to bring wagons to this galleon so they can be loaded with whiskey and rum and then taken back to Mickey's home and the Bounty. I do not want the Navy Commander to see how much is here."

I could see Mickey's eyes glisten and he said, "Yes Sir!" I said, "Please go back to the Bounty and get your staff and anyone else you know to be ready to off-load the cases of whiskey and rum. As soon as the wagons get back my crewmen will help you load them and then come back to the Bounty pub and load the wagons and take your horses back to Mickey's home. When your pub storage spaces are full, I will have the other crewmen deliver the remaining whiskey and rum from the galleon to my ship the Annabelle where I will store it for future trips and missions at sea."

I expect the Navy Admiral and his staff to be here in the afternoon to pay myself and the crew their percentage of the gold and silver coins and bars that were brought to Milford Haven on the trip prior to this whiskey and rum mission. I will give an accounting of the trip to Ireland. As promised, we will load his carriages and wagons with cases of whiskey and rum. So, you see, time is barely on our side.

I was amazed to see how fast Mickey and Aaron purchased those wagons and horses. You must know Mickey would only buy the best. He said, "They will make good resale stock!" There will probably not be many coins left out of Mickey's money bag after the end of that buying spree, so the remaining money will be added to the share of booty we must give to the commander of Naval Finance and Procurement.

I said, "Good job, but I am going to commandeer one of your wagons to transport whiskey and rom the Annabelle". The loading began and the wagons pulled out. There were two horses to a wagon and there were five wagons. He took four and I took one. I told them, "Those wagons and horses will belong to Aaron and he may sell them or rent them out." Aaron replied, "God Bless you Captain!"

Just as they had gone out of sight there came a wagon and carriages. After tying up the horses to the dock railing, the guards and their paymasters came sidling up the ramp showing as much authority as they could. The commander said, "Where did you find this? Never have there been four-masted Spanish galleon warships brought to English shores in such perfect condition. The few Spanish galleons that were brought back as booty were barely floating. So, I ask again…Where did you find it? How can this be?"

I said, "Sir, have you got a day or so that I might tell you the stories of how I commandeered this four-masted Spanish galleon? It is for you to know that there were losses of life, but none were of my crew!"

He looked at me and said, "You are a wonder sir!" I responded, "Remember sir, I achieved this with my warship and on my own time." I continued, "I was the captain of my own ship when I commandeered the galleon and all that is in as well as the other warships. Well, Admiral, I have twenty-five cases of Irish whiskey, twenty cases of scotch, and six barrels of rum that I promised you when you gave me time off to make a trip to the Irish coast for whiskey and rum. You may load this shipment at your leisure or my crew will help you load it. I will deliver to the English Naval yards the biggest and best Spanish galleon and also bring the cargo which has at least a million in British pounds of crystal, silver, utensils, pots and silver trays of tableware."

"Sir, in honor of your continued friendship, I will personally, along with my crewmen, deliver and sail the galleon under six British flags flown on the masts from bow to stern, and I will escort that ship with my Annabelle warship. I will do so in three days after you have time to notify all British ships at sea to <u>not</u> fire on what they know to be a Spanish ship of war! I will let you know now that I, Captain Joseph Worthy, totally reject the changes that you made in the contract where no bounty is given. I know you have on board your wagon, payment to myself and crew for the last booty we recently brought to you. I would please like that off-loaded from your wagons. I would like our share of the booty placed by the plank of the Annabelle". The paymaster commander said shortly after our words, "We will no longer pay the captains more for the use of the ship and wages to you and the crew! I do not have the authority to give you more. Your country needs the fortune to cover war expenses." After unloading our booty, I saw the commander board his carriage and turn it toward home with his own personal booty.

I bought a horse and carriage at the dock and proceeded as fast as possible to my home where Annabelle was waiting. I said, "Bring Will and we will go to your parent's home and I will tell you all of the adventures we just had!"

We rushed to Mickey's house and entered without knocking. We all took a chair and a portion of rum was poured for each and with wide eyes and mouth open, they listened to the adventures of the trip to Ireland, such as the buying of the whiskey and rom, and the taking of the Spanish galleon and pirate ship. Even after telling the story the questions seemed never to end. They wanted to know more and more. I finally said, "There will be more I can tell you tomorrow, but for now Annabelle and I would like to go home and retire." Aaron said, "I will give you an accounting of the whiskey and rum we took and its whereabouts." I said, "Don't bother! It's okay!"

I said, "I would tell you how much money we have but you would not be able to sleep. Do not speak to anyone about our booty!" I said goodnight to my precious family, grabbed Will in my arms and, along with Annabelle, headed home.

I said, "Annabelle, I didn't tell your parents about the riches I acquired on that trip, but eventually when we leave for the islands, we will leave plenty of it with your family. Annabelle, we need not worry about money the rest of our lives. Including all the money I have in the Bank and what I acquired from this adventure, we will have at least a minimum of three hundred million in English pounds! Right now, it is in boxes and treasure chests in my cabin on the Annabelle. Only my lieutenants know how much is there and they will be included in shares for their retirement. No one else knows of the wealth that we have stored on the Annabelle. I have a great crew of seamen, but if they become aware of that fortune they might turn to mutiny and theft. I have told my lieutenants to have the officers guard the ships to protect the silver and gold coin and bars. My hope is that they will guard that money with their lives. I will assign four warrior seamen to guard the area. Everyone thinks it was to protect the money that was left to us by the British Navy as booty. At a later time, that money will be divided among everyone.

I said, "When you come aboard, we will use the cabin adjoining my cabin from an inner door. This room is where the gold and silver is stored and stacked in there. The room was meant for my personal supplies. We must move many of these chests and boxes to the cabin adjoining mine to make room for you to live in."

Annabelle said, "Joseph, I am afraid to be alone! I am afraid when you set sail in that galleon and deliver it to the Naval Yard. Word might slip out from your lieutenants and I would be in danger—so would they---so would your son Will. We sat there for the longest time dwelling on the problem and what to do about it.

I thought carefully of each man on board and of how well I knew them and how trustworthy I thought they might be and how many men were aboard our three ships and what to do with them. It kept coming back to me that the danger still existed. It was an uneasy sleep that night for both of us. But, when the sun broke through the windows, I had a brilliant idea. I said, "Annabelle, I am going to do the very thing that I was afraid others would do to me!" Annabelle said, "Well…well what!" "Instead of giving the galleon, the Annabelle warship, and the treasure ship to England, I am going to take them to the west. We are going to set sail immediately. Everyone thinks that the Annabelle will be escorting the galleons east to the shipyards in southern England. Instead, I am going south out of the channel and then west across the Atlantic to the Americas. We will think about Cuba as a possible new home. I will secretly meet with my captains and tell them we are leaving Britain on sea duty, but I won't tell them what we are really doing. We will be a long way out to sea before any concern will arise as to why we are going west."

"Annabelle, we need to secretly get a large portion of gold and silver to your family before we leave. I plan on having the ship loaded with supplies tonight on all three ships. We will need wagons to secure our need for food and water. I don't want your parents to find out about our plan until well after we leave. Even they might let the "cat out of the bag" and we wouldn't be far enough out to sea to feel safe."

Again, we sat in a quandary. How would we pull that off? Of course, I would be leaving at least one million in the O'Hara's name so that your parents can share monies that they need. The money will be put in the London Bank. I announced, "Lets saddle up and ride down to the ship." My lieutenants informed me that all was well. I said, "I told you two lieutenants to come to my cabin with Annabelle and I. I am making a proposal to you. The day after tomorrow I want to have a full load of food supplies on all three ships. We are going to leave England to go to Havana, Cuba. Are you willing to do this? Are you married? Have girlfriends? Or don't want to leave? I am sailing from England for good. I am taking my ships and the booty with me too! Is there anyone here who cannot go? I am taking all three ships. You two will be captains. Skinner will be captain of the Spanish ship which we will call the Neptune. Captain John will be captain of the pirate ship which we will call the Horizon. You know there is about three ways to get the money now available. The twenty-five percent of the million which we were going to return to England, we are going to keep for ourselves. I am offering you millions of pounds with which to retire when you arrive at our destination. You will own twenty-five percent of that treasure which will ultimately be divided among you and the officers as needed. You will need to get the officers to go along with these ideas. I will, of course, maintain an accounting of all the rest of the millions in gold and silver to negotiate with the Cuban governor. Everything we have is in bullion coin or bars so it will be easy to disperse as I see fit."

I am sure Brittan and the Navy will consider us to have committed mutiny. But you must remember it is they who owe and who refuse to pay us for what we have done. We will not be receiving wages from

England. We must pay all crewmen from all three ships from the fortune we have on board. We can easily do this with the millions in silver and gold bars and stacks of British pounds that I have acquired. You will receive money whenever you want it. I will tell you now and later that we will pay for the fares on the merchant ships for your families' expenses to come to Cuba. We will tell no one until we are mid-Atlantic and we will make the same offer to the officers and crewmen that I have made to you today. We should not risk our lives in the Navy for the British for only wages. I will not risk our warship and our lives.

When we go to sea, we will tell the crewmen on all ships they may go back to Brittan on a merchant ship. I will hire merchant ships to transport those who wish to go back to Brittan or Ireland.

I said, "Lieutenants, leaving England for Havana has been in planning for several years. Now, the time is right! What you do not know is the other captains and myself have had difficulties in receiving our share of the booty. The Navy has been resisting and stating that we are getting too much and that England needs more in order to support the numerous war funds. They are committed to Asia, North Africa, and India being a critical one. They have told me that all booty must go to the Crown. The amount is just too large for them to agree to. The booty that was to go to the Navy, I am claiming to cover the amount owed to us for the renting of the Annabelle for the year, as well as my annual purse for my year of duty and your share as well.

I will tell the crewmen they will receive a bonus when we get to Cuba. Those that go back to England will receive much less. Right now, load the ships with enough provisions to get us to Havana. Be sure that there are more than enough barrels of water to sustain us on the voyage. Our supply officer knows how to calculate the amount of vegetables that are needed to be stored in the lower part of the ship where it is covered and the number of barrels of salt pork and beef that need to be stored as well. If the supply officer gets suspicious because of the quantity of provisions, just say we are going to need it on our lengthy mission. So, let's get busy gentlemen!"

I took the five wagons and horses I gave to Aaron and the crew started loading them at midnight, as always when it is cool, and there are fewer people "out and about". The people won't question our motives because the ship always loads at night. I said, "We will leave Sunday morning when the Milford Haven citizens are at church. Put everyone to work! There are a few dock workers you can hire too. The sooner we can get the galleon, the Annabelle, and the pirate ship loaded the easier it will be to get underway. Remember, we announced to the English commander that we will be transporting the galleon to the Naval yards under protection of the Annabelle, so when we leave everyone will think that is what we are doing. We will use the guns on the Spanish galleon if we are accosted by any Spanish warships or privateers."

Just before I departed, I met with Aaron and Annabelle's parents and told them to say nothing! We will not be coming back. One day we will return to get you or have you brought to us. Always be prepared to make the long trip. You should expect some reprisals. I want you to mail this sealed envelope to the British Navy that says if they, in any way, seek reprisal on my family, I will remove their ships at sea one-by-one, and build a Navy of my own. You know I can and I will do so. You examine the reasons why I am forced to do this.

Finally, I ordered the ships ropes released from the prior position on the dock and we quietly slipped out from the Milford Haven port into the Irish Sea at dawn. My lieutenants and officers used every one of the Spanish seamen to fill the necessary duties. Amazingly, the Spanish and English seamen all seemed not to think of each other as enemies. The bottom line is that I have one hundred twenty-five positions on each of the ships plus now we have one hundred twenty-five additional Spaniards to sail these three fine ships onto the high seas of the Atlantic. We had many more seamen on board than we needed, so no one had to do double duty. Everything was going fine until we reached the point where we should have turned the ships towards the eastern shores of England and the Navy yards.

When we turned the opposite direction, west toward Havana, the officers and a group of old "salts" starting yelling – "Wrong way--- Wrong way! – and getting a little bit nasty. Of course, they were not armed and we were…...just in case! I said, "How does it feel officers and crew to be a bunch of mutineers, and know that hanging is the ultimate punishment for mutiny?" That word was a frightening one. "Okay gentlemen, we are prepared to explain now---you cannot be considered mutineers because you are sailing on <u>my</u> ship and the galleon, which I took on my free time as you well know on that trip to Ireland, and the pirate ship as well. They are now <u>our</u> ships and we are <u>not</u> mutineers. We are now on our own. But I have funds to pay you double while you are at sea or on land with me. You do not know that the British Navy had stopped paying the bounty of booty to all of us. This is the monies you all looked forward to for retirement. We will do just fine on our own. Our captive Spanish ship commander and his crew will be released and given their freedom. I have hired some of the skilled Spanish crewmen to sail under my command. The rest will be allowed to sign with other Spanish merchant ships. Some just want to find work when we get to Cuba. You and every seaman aboard may remain a member of my crew for which you will continue to receive double wages and bonuses as long as you are a crewman on one of our three warships. You will receive these wages at the end of each voyage. Lieutenant John, go to the Spanish and bring to the office two of their key officers. Go immediately, and bring them to my cabin."

When they came to the deck, we found them to be well qualified Spanish officers. I told them both, "I want you all to listen to my proposal to you. You are going to Havana, Cuba. There you will be give your freedom. If you are qualified, you may become crew members of one of the three ships and receive double the pay you are now getting."

My officers brought the Spanish officers into the cabin and gave them each a portion of rum. I said, "Officers we have left England permanently. We have taken the booty, the pirate ship, the Annabelle and the Spanish galleon with us. I can guarantee that I have a fortune that I have earned throughout my years of service and can easily meet all my financial promises. You may tell the Spanish officers and seamen that I will give them their freedom when we get to Havana if they so choose, and you as well.

The Spanish officers and you can find another passage to anywhere or be hired on another ship. This is a decision I made today. I dismissed the Spanish officers and then told my English officers that they may have the same opportunity." All of the officers agreed to the conditions. I said, "Make it clear to all of our current crew that we have hired that they will continue to receive double wages as long as they remain crew members on all my ships both at sea and land."

"Lieutenants, if we need more money or coin to satisfy the specialists aboard, we will decide how much and give it to them. Do not just spend what we have! What do you think gentlemen? Do you like these ideas?" They all said, "Indeed we do!" and nearly shook my hand off at the wrist. I said, "Our paymaster will see to it that everyone will be paid a fair wage and the crewmen will receive fifty pounds in bonuses. But not until we reach our destination of Havana, Cuba. So now officers it is your turn to get excited!

Throughout the years you will receive an equal share of the millions in Spanish bars that are mine from my service. Cash disbursements will be made to you each month based on your needs. This will last you a lifetime. Before you tell the seamen of the booty they are to receive, you will need to meet and decide how much money to give the specially trained seamen and how much you will give the others. However, I am ordering you to equally share enough money for each of you to retire before dispensing any money. I will be keeping a substantial sum in gold and silver bars and coin for my family and for what I earned over twenty years of service. If things go according to plan, I will be building a bank in Cuba and will put millions into that bank to make loans and receive interest. Lieutenants, I wish for you to accompany the officers and meet with the seamen and explain in detail what I have told you and there will be more than ample funds to live on for themselves and family when they get to Havana, Cuba.

If the seamen and officers wish to return to England, they will receive one thousand pounds in British money and that is all. In Cuba I will hire a merchant ship to accommodate any man who wishes to <u>not</u> proceed on this adventure. They will return you to Ireland or Denmark or France or you may go back to England. Choose your own path!" If any officer changes their mind when we get to Cuba, you may join the others that wish to return home with only one silver bar. If you stay as a member of my crew you and your family will receive enough money to live on the rest of your lives. As the money I have increases in our bank investment, you all will share in the dividends received. I said, "Men, we are bound for Havana, Cuba and your riches will be much greater than those that left us."

Annabelle stroked my back and said, "Oh my captain, I am so proud of you!" I looked into her eyes and was grateful for those words. It was agreed upon from the very beginning that my dear Annabelle should show no physical affection of any kind in front of any and all men on board.

It was not long before we were seeing many small islands leading into that sea. There was no privateer that dared to attempt to challenge a four-masted warship. We were positioned to support each other. It was so tempting to anchor near one of these islands and visit them. My lieutenant gave advice in saying, "Sir, may we please proceed straight to Havana, Cuba without stops.' I agreed.

I had the foresight to replace the Spanish flags with the English flags, or we would be considered the enemy. We anchored some distance from the Havana port and I sent Lieutenant John in a skiff to that port to make arrangements for long-term mooring. Of course, I sent ample coin to persuade the port officials to find and grant their requests. After displaying Captain Joseph's papers as owner of the four-masted galleon and the four-masted Annabelle, I was given written consent for entrance and docking privileges to the famous port.

They allowed my third warship to enter as well. They felt overwhelmed at the small armada I was bringing to the port. Our three warships entered the very large port and anchored facing three directions.

After anchoring I, along with two of my lieutenants, boarded our skiff with two crewmen who rowed us to the dock. I met with the dock officials and the military guard and asked to see the governor on very important business. They, too, after looking at me and my three warships, decided that it would be okay and approved the visit. He sent an official to the governor's palace to request an audience. That man soon returned and said, "By all means, come with me!"

After climbing many stairs and steps, we came to his ornate office. His servants opened the doors and invited us in. The governor stared intently at me and said, "I see your warships. What is your purpose?" I said, Governor Madarrga, I am here to make you President of your own country. You are now President Madarrga. You never again will be taken advantage of and ruled by Spain. You will now make your own decisions for you and your country. England will be your protector, and me and my three warships will patrol your waters against pirates of which there are plenty, and see to it that Spanish warships will not come within miles of your shore, except for their merchant ships wanting to purchase goods from you. You may keep your dependable staff and friends, but if Spain has any of their officers or men here to control you, they must be terminated in any way you so choose. I suggest shipping them to one of the adjacent islands. If we find any alien Spanish men that you are not aware of, we will dispose of them in the same way. I expect you to turn over the military you have to us. I will place millions in gold and silver coin and bars in a new bank that I will build. The bank will be for you and your business from which to borrow at a fair interest rate. We will build a large bank from which you will receive a share of the profits. These are only two of the many things that I will do. I will not take orders from you, but will support and see to it that the decisions you make will happen. We will have a merchant ship bring the new Martin Luther Printing Press to Cuba so that your word and directives can be printed so all may read them.

If we overreach our protectorant of authority, you will let us know the changes you would like to make. Ultimately, you will be a very rich president from the taxes from the new businesses that I will help finance. As Havana grows and the country grows, you will have more wealth than you probably know what to do with. Do we have an agreement then?"

Madarrga stared at me for the longest time and he looked out the window at the warships and stared at me again and said, "Yes, Captain Worthy! He smiled and said, by all means Captain Joseph, we have an arrangement."

I said, "Mr. President, you have made your son and your sons' son very happy people, for I am sure that in the future they will follow in your foot steps as President. Sir, you have a country!" Madarrga was a short, bearded fellow and he seemed to me to an honest man.

After this meeting, I left President Madarrga's office and I and my captains toured the harbor. Notices were spread by word and by written signs that no citizen of Havana will in any way in the future be in danger of losing their life or possessions. I passed the word out to all that they would continue their lives as they had been enjoying them. Your country is now a protectorant of England.

There are many businesses in the beautiful Havana waterfront. I offered to buy them all and asked them to continue managing them and share in the profits with myself and pay taxes. Some of the small businesses which were successful refused the offer and I let them. I told every business owner they may borrow from the new bank of Cuba for funds that they need to operate their businesses, but must pay interest on that loan. Waterfront security for all businesses will be paid for and provided by your Cuban government from the taxes you pay. President Madarraga sent notice to all that everyone, according to their income, will pay taxes.

After the lieutenants and other officers carefully explained to the men the benefits of being in Cuba, they rallied and then seemed to be ecstatic knowing that they would receive a home that was paid for from the treasures of their warship sea battles. My wife Annabelle and I were so happy because they had the many skills that they could apply to their businesses.

The President was happy as well. I now told the President we would have to agree to one more important part of these agreements. Again, I asked for housing for my crewmen. Their wives and families will arrive in Havana to join them and until the new houses are built, they will need funding. Madarrga said, "Oh, yes, we will pay for accommodations, including cost of their meals at restaurants." I knew that many single crewmen would have to live on board ship until the housing was completed for there are not that many available hotels where they can be accommodated. This situation could last for one year or more. Please consider the inclusion of maintenance and daily clean-up. I told the President I would sail the four-masted galleon and would anchor one of my four-masted warships in the harbor, and with cannons pointed towards the entrance of the harbor, I would protect Cuba from all oncoming ships who might have devious thoughts. I will see to it that no enemy ship will pillage this port at any time. This ship, within ten months from now, will be joined by two more British ships to patrol the perimeter of your country. Merchant ships will be allowed to enter your ports. I sent the message to the Cuban President and soon he agreed in writing to all of the conditions. I sent another message to the Cuban

President indicating that I may take my ship the Annabelle to England. Before I do, I will replace my two warships with two other warships which will continue to protect the islands. Before I leave, I expect that England will bring a warship to protect Cuba. You will consider them my ships, but in your service, to protect your country.

Never have we enjoyed such beautiful balmy breezes and good weather day after day. It was great fun for us to watch the growth of the building on the waterfront and harbor. The Cubans created successful businesses. I deposited millions in coin and bars into the new Cuban Bank. The bank is only two stories but had vaults to protect all monies. It was strange seeing some of my ex-crewmen dressed in fine business suits as they learned the banking business.

Annabelle and I enjoyed walking that waterfront dock and listening to the greeting of those men who now had new lives. Gradually we saw more and more of them in the company of Spanish ladies. It was good to see the Spanish captors with their freedom from us. I had to acquire more seamen to fill the positions on my three warships while the others were taking shore leave.

I sent notices to all Cubans that they could deposit money in the new bank and it would be protected and they would earn dividends on those deposits or they could borrow money and pay interest.

Annabelle was working in our garden when one of my ex-crewmen came dashing through the garden gate gasping for air from the long run. He said, Captain, Captain, there are two huge four-masted warships that are requesting to anchor off shore!" They anchored outside the port entrance and sent a small boat to meet with me.

The English Admiral said, "I am required to meet with you at your leisure." I replied, "Of course!" I told the messenger that my wife Annabelle and I would meet with him and his lieutenants at tea time or about three o'clock the next day at our home. I asked, "Do you know the nature of the requested visit?" He replied, "Not shared with me Sir! I will be leaving to return the message to the admiral right away!"

Annabelle and I were never more curious as to why a ship of the Royal Navy would make such a journey to speak to a captain that had deserted with a four-masted galleon and two other warships they believed should have been theirs.

We were dressed in our fineries. I wore my dress uniform and my side-arms. Annabelle wore her finest dress. Soon they came---The Admiral and his staff of three.

I said, "Now gentlemen, other than trying to arrest me, I can't imagine why England would send noblemen and officers of high rank to meet with me." The Admiral said, "We are here per directives of the Crown and the Navy Admirals to exonerate you from all the claims we made against you when you left. We also want to make you a Master Commander of the three ships and these papers show that you are Master Commander of all three "A-1" classified warships. We found out from a merchant ship that you have made Britain a protectorant of Cuba and made the Governor the President of Cuba. We discovered you were using the warships to protect the harbor and the perimeter of Cuba's island country. We are proud of you and you may return to England any time you choose. I was ecstatic at hearing these official words and I accepted those promotions to Master Commander and letters from the Crown and one from the Navy. There was also a letter from Parliament giving me praise for my conquests.

The Admiral said, "I have brought you a golden box with a golden stamp and seal for President Madarrga. His name is embossed so he may give an official stamp to all of his documents and letters." I said, "I would be proud to present it to him unless you wish to do so?" Representative Beasley replied, "No, this is for you to do. We have other missions to accomplish." I said to them, "I am really sorry to tell you I have to cancel your other missions in order to make this protection arrangement agreement to provide two additional warships to protect their island of Cuba. I contacted the President and told them you would be bringing the warships and indeed you have. Within the next day or two, I am returning to England to take you home."

I continued, "I will pay the Crown one million in British pounds for these ships. I know that they will think that keeping my promises to the President is a good investment. Britain and its merchant ships will be happy to know that you will now have free trade with Cuba and not to worry about being preyed upon by Spanish warships or privateers. No one will even consider this because of the five-warship armada in this area. Captain Beasley and his captain of the other warship, Captain Belford said in unison, "This has been part of the plan to have the British as protectorant of Cuba."

I said, "I am giving you this sum of money to pacify any English officer who cares to disagree. Now sirs, sit with me and we will have some Cuban rum and I will personally escort you to the hotel where you will stay until we return to England. Your English crewmen aboard the two warships may continue to be crewmen in their jobs at double their pay. Those who do not wish to remain in their current jobs may return with us on the Annabelle to England. You may be surprised how many will wish to stay on."

Lieutenant Skinner will accompany you and Captain Belford to the hotel and notify your crewmen as to why the ships are remaining and that the captains and officers will be taken back home by Master Commander Joseph Worthy. When these crews heard of double wages all but twenty-five crewmen on the ships chose to stay on their ships. I could accommodate these twenty-five crewmen when we return to England in a few days.

You may tell them that accommodations will be made for their room and board and I will share the cost of bringing their families as well as having houses built for them if they choose to stay. Captain Beasley said, "I guess this is why you are negotiating with the President of Cuba. You have caused Britain to be the protectorant of Cuba." I said, "On the way back, I will see to it that you have a bountiful supply of Cuban rum and boxes of cigars to give you some relief at this completion of agreements. I have three letters now, one from Parliament, one from the Crown, and one from the Naval Commander, that I will present to President Madarrga.

I said, "During the two days in waiting for the voyage home, you may take a tour of the harbor businesses and bars and listen to their splendid singing and music. Consider it a short vacation."

No salutes were given---just nods. I said, "We will put you up in a Cuban hotel until we leave in two days and we will pay for the lodging. By the way, this harbor is called Annabelle Harbor for those that are making the maps back home. We will leave at dawn on the third day, this being the first day."

It was a sight to see----The Cuban President and his entourage hurrying down the palace steps. President Madarrga saw that there were two additional warships. He said, "Captain, what have you done?" I said, "Just as I planned, there will be five four-masted warships to protect you with six hundred fifteen cannons that will protect the waters around Cuba and one to remain in the harbor at all times."

I said, "Never fear, Mr. President, I have observed over a period of time that you are a great leader! I expect your son and your sons' son to become a long line of Madarrga Presidents. As England is your protectorant, they wish you to be loved by your countrymen and never e feared.

To begin with, surround yourself with skilled members of your staff. Your people now want you to give them water wells, more roads, and roads that are lit by more lanterns, and they want better schools and bigger and better hospitals with trained doctors and nurses. They want more smoke houses to protect meats and fish. They want more and better sewage drains. They want a bigger police force to protect them without abusing its power.

We still have a dire need for at least eight hundred homes for our crewmen and officers near the harbor. I will need help in securing builders from your country and any other country or the Dominican Republic where you have good relations." He said, "Oh yes, Master Commander Joseph Worthy, which I hear is your new title! I will see to it that your requests are honored as you have honored mine."

I said, "Mr. Madarrga, this is just a partial list of their needs. Your job as President is to direct the right people to accomplish these things. This is what will make you a loved President. As Commander of your land and sea battles and infantry, we will see that you get the support you will need to ensure these assignments are completed to you and your people's satisfaction."

The President said to me, "You are to be considered our country's hero, and I will place our security men and four warriors under your command. Please train them as well as you have trained yours."

Again, in that very courtyard, there was singing and dancing and they enjoyed the rum as well. All of Havana, Cuba celebrated this historical event.

Now the work begins. I brought together the most insightful crewmen and other business leaders to meet jointly with each other and members of the English crews that also arrived. I announced to all of the crewmen that they must help us decide where and what their skills were, other than on a ship. As Master and Commander of all military forces, I, Captain Joseph, am telling you, "I, and my many officers will see to it that you have an opportunity to pursue your skills. This will take some time. Gentlemen, during your interviews, we will house and feed you well from the galleys of all five warships and from on shore eateries. Only designated crewmen will be allowed to possess firearms. Ultimately, as we find competent men to police the island, they will then be the ones permitted to carry firearms.

As we speak, there are schooners being boarded by young to middle-aged ladies from Norway, Finland, Scotland and Ireland and the Isle of the Caribbean to join Cuba and its wonderful quality of life. They wish to come to Cuba for a new life. I am sure many of you would like to pursue a love affair and perhaps marry. Among them will be singers and dancers to work at the newly built entertainment center. They will be here in a week or two.

Just a reminder to be neat and clean in appearance when you are interviewed. You may have to change your ways. All crewmen from the English warships will be interviewed by Havana's businessmen to determine where their skills could best be applied. We will place those with fewer skills in an apprenticeship in a skill that they could learn easily, and like as well. The following are some positions that might be of interest: Growing tobacco, rolling cigars, farm work, sugar plantations, distilling rum, cattle rancher, or working on fishing boats. Time and training will depend on the skills you to choose to learn.

In fact, at the end of that time, and if you still wish to return to England, one of our several merchant ships will be hired to take you home. If you stay you will be free to stay with the person you work with or find a business of your own somewhere in Cuba. This country needs skills of all types and people too. We have hotel people, merchants, and entertainers to be among the most sought-after skills at this moment. Remember this---Cuba is a country of its own under the protection of my five four-masted warships and their captains, which have the capability to protect you. I also want to inform everyone that we are seeking to commandeer vessels that are further out to sea and bring them back to Cuba as prizes. We do not want war, but are more than capable of defeating any ship and bringing it back to the Cuban shipyards.

President Madarrga will speak to you often and send posted notices on the new printing press on the progress and state of your country.

For those of you with families, we will secure passage for them to join you in Cuba. We will use merchant ships from here or other countries and pay the captains when your families are brought safely to Cuba. Remember, you will be well paid in the skill you achieve. This is a popular resort country with great wealth and the tourists pay well for the things that you create. Interviewing will start immediately and those hired will start working at their apprenticeships tomorrow.

You are not free from the English Naval. Until you resign, you will live by English rules and Cuban laws. You will report to your English officers at the time they request. Remember all of you eight hundred crewmen and many officers, you are still members of the Navy and have responsibilities to your captains, your fellow crewmen, your families and your country of Cuba. Have I told you that since the English officers brought the final two ships, that the British patrol and commander of the Navy reinstated regular Navy wages to everyone and I will make up the rest. Finally, the island of Cuba is now an independent country under the protection of England with Mr. Madarrga as your President.

It wasn't long before another English ship made its way to this paradise. It was here for a two-fold purpose. The first was a letter from the King that states that My new title will be Sir Joseph Worthy, Ambassador of Cuba. It went on to say how proud England was that I had secured another protectorant country. The second purpose of this visit was to meet with the new President of Cuba and assure him that the English would forever be the protectorant of his country and be a valuable asset in trading, and also, they should not worry about Spain and other countries pirating Cuba. England's new Ambassador, Sir Joseph Worthy, will keep the English Crown informed of your needs and ours.

I hurried off to see Annabelle and my son Will and showed them the documents from the crown and asked, "Do you think your parents and

Aaron and his family would join us here? Annabelle, with the approval of the English Crown, we will go back to England to bring your family to Cuba. When we return, we will build them a fine new house near us." Annabelle was overjoyed at the thought. She said, "Oh, do you think my parents will come with us back to Havana?" I replied, "We will soon find out."

The greatest event ever occurred on the way back to England. Annabelle said, "This reminds me of another night when we slept together." Her face turned quickly towards mine and mine toward hers and I said, "What?" Annabelle said in the softest words I ever heard, "Joseph, I am with child again!" We turned our bodies toward each other. I pulled her close to me and I said, "Thank you." It was all I could do to keep from whimpering like a child. I told her I was very happy!

We soon heard "Land Ho!" When we pulled into port Milford Haven there were many people at the dock to greet us, including the leader of the English Parliament and the Navy Admiral. The officers, Beasley and Belford, from when we commandeered the warship in Cuba, were happy to be back, saluted and left.

It was a pleasant trip. We had much to do on arrival. Aaron had married Annabelle's Irish girlfriend, Ida Lee. The Bounty pub had made them rich. They had a vast number of friends there and their two children were doing wonderfully well in school. Her brother Aaron hugged his sister Annabelle and looked at me and said, "We could never do better or be happier than we are right now in Milford Haven." I said, "We may not ever see each other again, but we will stay in touch by mail. Every ship departing here for Cuba delivers mail now for there are many Englishmen in Cuba. We will stay in touch!" Oh, how the tears did flow.

Mickey and Anne jumped at the chance to make the trip. Like me, they had always been adventuresome and wanted so badly to be near Will while he grew up. I told Annabelle, Mickey and Anne when we get back to Cuba, we will build a home to their liking and they will be close to our home.

Aaron said jokingly, "Joseph, remember those horses you gave to me? We have a horse farm now as well. It is kind of our hobby. We buy, sell, train and race them."

Mickey and Anne, with the help of Aaron, loaded all of the O'Hara's belongings in both wagons. This included equipment from Mickey's gun repair shop. Also loaded were his hand-hewn chairs and an abundance of boxes of Irish whiskey which he still had stored everywhere in his home. I said, "Mickey, I can't believe you will ever run out of whiskey, but if you do, I will take care of it." Then Mickey did his cute little Irish jig. I said, "Such a happy man he is." Finally, everything was aboard and we weighed anchor the next morning for the journey back to Cuba. What an adventure!

We left port Milford Haven with the Annabelle leading the way. It was late and Annabelle's parents went to bed in my captain's quarters. I had taken Annabelle to the bow of the ship and we stood there facing the West and held hands. Momentarily, I felt a tug on my waistcoat and there was little Will Worthy. He looked up at me and said, "I am ready for my duty, Sir!" I had never heard Will say these words to me. I looked at him and said, "Will, you have an important job as co-lookout. While you are on duty, I am your captain and you may address me as Captain, Sir. You may salute me and address me as Captain." Will said, "Yes". Then I showed him how to salute. I said, "Lets try it again seaman." I turned back and looked at Annabelle and then back to the sea. I said, "Do it again seaman Will! This time salute me." Then Will said, "Captain, Sir, what is my duty tonight? Will I be at the stern of the ship? He added, Dad, where is the stern?" I said, "Seaman, go to the opposite direction and go to the other end of the ship and you will report to that officer. You will be co-lookout. He will show you and train you as to what to do." Later, I heard that my seaman Will called to the co-lookout captain and saluted when he met the officer.

Annabelle and I stood there at the bow chuckling about what we had just experienced with Will. We turned with our hands on the rail facing West. I put my arm around her and she put her arm around my waistcoat. There was a huge bright full moon doing its best to drown out the beauty of the endless sea of stars. The waves were small and caressing the bow with a slapping sound at every movement of the ship.

Her Majesty had delivered to me a golden presidential hand sealed box with Madarrga's name embossed on it to be presented to him on our arrival in Cuba.

The trip home was uneventful, but very long. Finally, my ship the Annabelle sailed into Annabelle Harbor in Havana, Cuba. We moored at our own dock and stepped off of the boarding plank as Madarrga himself waved and saluted me while a mariachi band started to play. I hurriedly walked up to Madarrga with Annabelle on my arm and saluted him in return and said, "What an honor! I can hardly believe this greeting!" Madarrga said, "It is well deserved Master Commander Joseph Worthy!" Annabelle was holding the golden box. She curtsied and said, "This is from the Crown of England, with their blessings!" He took the box that contained the embossed stamp with his name on the bottom and thanked her. I swear, I saw tears in his eyes, but Presidents don't cry, do they?

There was merriment on the dock and guitar playing and singing. After I introduced Mickey and Anne, Annabelle's parents, to our President Madarrga, they were escorted to a carriage and delivered to our home. Annabelle and I boarded another carriage that Madarrga offered and we were then taken to our home as well. Of course, Mickey insisted that one box of Irish whiskey be delivered to our home as well.

I cannot say that this is the end of this narrative for there is another adventure awaiting us in Havana. My son, Will, and I do our tour of duty at sea. One day he too will be a captain of his own ship. Will must tour and be adventuresome going to the other islands along the coast of the Americas and up the rivers. But the story, as the generations of Worthy's go, will be a never-ending one. I have y regrets and self-doubt because of the battles and deaths that were a part of the wars at sea. However, happiness and gratefulness prevails!

Joseph and Annabelle Worthy

William Milborn

The following are the men who chose to be pirates for their country, or for power, or for treasures.

Many of these pirates were vanquished by my grandfather Eric Worthy, my father Alexander Worthy, or myself, Joseph Worthy. The majority of the pirates, as yet, I have not faced in battle.

I have indicated on the map in this book the places at sea where my grandfather, my father and myself had our victories at sea. They are depicted by small ships marking their positions at sea.

The following is a list of some of the pirates from many different countries that roamed the seas:

Roberts	Hawkins
LaFayette	Love
LaFeet	North
Drake	Raleigh
Bontemps	Black Beard
Johnson	Roberval
Morgan	

Epilogue

Since the publication of the adventure there have been so many things happening to the Worthy's, I need to write a sequel. First, there has been a horrendous misfortune happen to the Worthy family and how we managed to overcome it. There have been problems with the Cuban President Madarrga as he has begun to flex his muscles toward me and others and how I dealt with it. I will want to tell you of the adventures that my wife, my son Will, and my warship Annabelle will have when we patrol the islands with our warship Neptune. We will patrol around the islands surrounding Cuba and the Dominican Republic, Jamaica and the shores of Panama and Mexico, Texas and Florida, as well as the western shores of America. You will find in the future book, how Annabelle has continued her career as a singer and dancer at the new casino. I want to tell you what her Irish mother and father (Anne and Mickey) are up to in their new adventures.

In Cuba there has been another major battle when our crew fights with the pirate Captain Morgan. There will be other sea battles. This is the primary place where pirates lurk to do their bidding.

I need to tell you that since Annabelle and I have settled in Havana, I have taken my ship the Annabelle out to sea a number of times along with my son Will. On one journey that sticks in my mind is when I returned to Ireland and then to England with one of my best warships captained by John, I witnessed a view that will be emblazoned in my mind.

We traveled by way of the North shore of Ireland and England where we viewed the mass of skeletons of ships along the shore that had been previously lost in battle with another warship or Mother Nature. There were many masts protruding above the water along the shoreline. Some probably had been sunk by jagged rocks tearing open their lower hulls. There were ragged sail cloths hanging from the yardarms where once there were beautiful sails. All this, I say to you, is a testimony to the dangers that the men with their sailing ships face on the high seas.

Our trip was to pick up Irish whiskey and then visit Aaron O'Hara, Annabelle's brother in Milford Haven, England and to see if he had needs or wanted to join the rest of the family in Havana, Cuba.

Finally, you will learn of Will Worthy's training to be a seaman with me as I did with my father and my father did with his father. Already, there are funny tales to tell about his seaman training!

Printed in the United States
By Bookmasters